THE PALE BROWN THING

The
Pale Brown
Thing

by

Fritz Leiber

Swan River Press
Dublin, Ireland
MMXXII

The Pale Brown Thing
by Fritz Leiber

Published by
Swan River Press
Dublin, Ireland
in February MMXXII

www.swanriverpress.ie
brian@swanriverpress.ie

"Thibaut de Castries" © Donald Sidney-Fryer
The Pale Brown Thing © Estate of Fritz Leiber
This edition © Swan River Press

Cover design by Meggan Kehrli from
"And Waved at Him" (2016) by Jason Zerrillo.

Typeset in Garamond by Ken Mackenzie

Paperback Edition
ISBN 978-1-78380-761-1

Swan River Press published
a limited edition hardback of
The Pale Brown Thing
in July 2016.

Contents

Thibaut de Castries, Revenant

R e-reading the modern classic novel of supernatural terror *Our Lady of Darkness* in its original form as *The Pale Brown Thing*—published in two parts in the January and February issues for 1977 by *The Magazine of Fantasy and Science Fiction*—the student of its author receives ample proof of not just his innate superiority as a veteran fictioneer but, what is more, of how much Fritz Leiber wrote as a realist, albeit always with imaginative overtones.

A case in point, *The Pale Brown Thing* furnishes us with a perfect example of both his imaginative realism and the manner to which he extrapolated fiction out of his immediate life and environment, such as it was at that time, in this instance, the San Francisco of the late 1960s through the early 1990s, until his death on 5 September 1992 at almost a full eighty-two years—he had been born on 24 December 1910. The novel in question very much reflects, and amiably so, the Hippie Period that flourished in "the City" during 1965 through 1975, and then lingered in some form or fashion for some yet further time.

Shortly after the death of Jonquil, his wife of many years, Fritz moved to San Francisco during the Christmas season of 1969, with the assistance of a few close friends, including Margo Skinner, Gloria Kathleen Braly, and myself, Donald Sidney-Fryer (the latter two had just married), driving north from Los Angeles (from Venice to the South of Santa

Monica) and its western littoral on the Pacific Ocean. Later he retrieved his possessions from his former coastal residence near the so-called Boardwalk.

At first Fritz stayed for a while with friends, but as soon as he recovered from his prolonged grief over Jonquil's death (and concomitant alcoholic daze), he found his own residence. He settled in a small apartment in the same building and on the same floor as Margo Skinner, who for years typed up the final versions of his manuscripts. The small apartment in question was located in downtown San Francisco, at 811 Geary Avenue (the former Rhodes Hotel), just as described in *The Pale Brown Thing*. This building and its neighborhood figure with especial flair in both that short novel and its final incarnation, the somewhat revised and expanded *Our Lady of Darkness*.

Our Lady of Darkness, Mater Tenebrarum, the mother of utter gloom and profoundest night, the manifestation of the utter lack of light, indeed!—who makes a terrifying and unforgettable appearance in the course of the novel.

Without exactly being a *roman à clef*, both versions of this hyper-natural or "paranormal" story closely reflect real people and real places; that is downtown San Francisco and Corona Heights, with the Junior Museum nearby, to the northwest of the major intersection of Market and Castro Streets.

Fritz has assuredly rounded up a grand and fascinating cast of characters for his at first contemplative and then fast-moving narrative. He adumbrates himself as the writer of supernatural-horror fiction, Franz Westen; and, although deceased, Jonquil is also present in the story as Daisy, Westen's late wife. He based sister and brother Dorotea and Fernando Luque, both from Peru, on the then-manager of 811 Geary Avenue and her sibling. However, the young harpsichordist Calpurnia, is not the shadow of

Fritz's close friend Margo Skinner as might be supposed; instead, he based Cal on some other person, a musician who had lived in the same building. Finally, the essential, or quintessential books that Franz has piled along the inner edge of his bed (flush with the wall), which he dubs the "Scholar's Mistress", becomes a real person (however briefly) in the course of the narrative.

These people become the *dramatis personae* that animate the overarching narrative, that of the author's San Francisco of the early and middle 1970s. Meanwhile, in counterpoint to this plot, Fritz has another narrative happening in the background, an historical one involving Ambrose Bierce, George Sterling, Jack London, Nora May French, and Clark Ashton Smith.

Clark Ashton Smith was living near Auburn during the late 1920s, but sojourned on occasion in "the City" following the death of George Sterling, his great mentor, in November of 1926. Between then and 1930, graduating from his poems in prose composed between 1912 and 1929, Smith began writing his mature short stories, whether fantasy or science fiction, and finished a dozen or more by 1930. Fritz cleverly and implicitly suggests that during one of these trips to San Francisco Smith had an encounter that may have inspired much of his later fiction. Who knows? But it is a wonderful and creative gambit!

The main and most mysterious character in the historical counter-narrative is a certain Thibaut de Castries. An intriguing name, de Castries was possibly based in part on Adolphe de Castro, otherwise known as Gustav Adolf Danziger (1859-1959). With this gentleman, Ambrose Bierce collaborated on the short novel *The Monk and the Hangman's Daughter*, first published in the *San Francisco Examiner* in September 1891. Some data concerning this novel are in order here.

Bierce was first introduced to de Castro in 1886 by their mutual acquaintance Petey Bigelow. De Castro, then a twenty-three year old German Jew, formerly a rabbi, a lawyer, and then a dentist, is described as a "buzzing little gadfly" in Paul Fatout's excellent 1951 biography of Bierce. De Castro had made a rough translation of Richard Voss's *Der Mönch von Berchtesgaden*, first published in the German monthly magazine *Vom Fels zum Meer* (1890-1), which Bierce re-wrote into much better English, also reshaping the narrative and including the surprise ending.

The Monk and the Hangman's Daughter tells the story of the monk Ambrosius, who murders his loved one to prevent her from marrying someone else, the plot thus another variant of the Eternal Triangle. Although critic Clifton Fadiman thought that it lacked Bierce's characteristic voice, the translated novel remains a vivid, effective and colorful opus; and also a rather grim one, like so much of everyday life during the Middle Ages in Europe. While all of this may not seem immediately germane to *The Pale Brown Thing*, Fritz had read much of Bierce's output in depth, including this unique novel spawned between de Castro and "old man" Bierce. Something of the narrative might very well have entered into Thibaut de Castries' dangerous and enigmatic personality—especially the black magick secreted somehow into his published monograph, *Megapolisomancy*, and the curious journal probably written by Smith, inspired by his brief but close acquaintance with Thibaut.

Thanks to the certain black magick set in place by Thibaut before he died, embittered somehow by his encounter with the Auburn poet and fictioneer, a subtle curse against Smith goes into operation against Franz Westen when he by chance activates the dormant sorcery. Once things get started in *The Pale Brown Thing*'s chief narrative, they happen with exemplary speed, as they do in Fritz's earlier, and now classic, supernatural novel *Conjure Wife*, the latter taking place in the late 1930s or early 1940s. Even though his entire career is marked by exceptional books—from his first collection of stories *Night's Black Agents* (Arkham House, 1947) to his monumental science-fiction novel *The Wanderer* in 1964—it is easy to overlook just what an outstanding writer Fritz Leiber had become by the late 1970s.

In any of the fictional narratives that he develops, Fritz describes his major or minor characters with great care and cunning, and plants his clues and portents with no less expertise. We have not yet mentioned one of the most notable characters in *The Pale Brown Thing*, as notable as Franz Westen in the present or Thibaut de Castries in the past. This character is Jaime Donaldus Byers, who serves as the major bridge between the modern narrative and the historical plot of the late 1890s.

Fritz based this character on selected aspects of the present writer, Donald Sidney-Fryer. And Fritz does very nicely by him! Donaldus Byers, a bisexual, resides with a female companion, and exotic Chinese, a live-in partner and mistress, in a restored two-story Victorian house on Beaver Street, going west upward to Buena Vista Park on one of the minor side streets off Castro Street, not far from the major intersection at Haight Street and Castro. Byers is apparently well-off in a financial sense, and exists in the story as a dilettante and connoisseur—one who has an insider's knowledge of Thibaut. He does not share this information at once with Franz, and not until the latter becomes more deeply involved in *l'affaire* Thibaut as associated with Smith does Byers become more forthcoming.

It is true that Sidney-Fryer lived in San Francisco during the Hippie Period (again, at its most flourishing, basically the years 1965-1975), and was a practicing bisexual or rather trisexual—that is, try anything sexual with human beings. And it is true that he had friends living in a Victorian house on the south side of Beaver Street, where he entertained lovers on various occasions. During the late 1960s and the early 1970s he was married to Gloria Kathleen Braly, and after several years of domestic bliss, they divorced, but remained friends. He was also an artist-writer-poet-performer. Far from being well-off, he worked at and maintained a part-time business, lived simply and frugally, and, after ten years' labor, completed and had caused to be published by Arkham House, the first series of *Songs and Sonnets Atlantean* (1971), shortly after which the owner-editor of Arkham House, August Derleth, passed on.

The historical narrative involving Thibaut de Castries, and other characters less fictional from *fin-de-siècle* San Francisco, does in fact reflect Fritz's own long-term fascination with Bierce, George Sterling, Jack London, Nora May French, Herman Scheffauer, and (last but not least) Clark Ashton Smith, as he became associated, albeit marginally, with the group via his mentor Sterling. But *The Pale Brown Thing* also reflects Fritz's long-term friendship with Sidney-Fryer, and the latter's insistent and persistent interest in the same group of writers, Clark Ashton Smith above all.

Sidney-Fryer began his own writing career as a scholar expounding in a series of essays on Smith as well as others in this group, subsequently identified as the California Romantics. These pieces were collected much later (along with others) in the volume *The Golden State Phantasticks* (2012). All during the composition of these essays, beginning in the early 1960s, Fritz and Sidney-Fryer had many intensive discussions concerning the California Romantics, their world, and their diverse literary productions.

It is indeed uncanny to what extent all, or most of, the characters and locations in this early version of *Our Lady of*

Darkness parallel or echo real people and real places without becoming fictional stand-ins or substitutes—so close they are to the real things! However, more than this, *The Pale Brown Thing* does capture to perfection the atmosphere of San Francisco during the Hippie Period. But, as he did so in life, Fritz handles the hippies with respect, gentleness and love, recognizing in them free spirits akin to his own.

We may doubt whether Fritz and Margo would recognize today the over-all downtown district of San Francisco, so many and so lofty have the high-rise edifices become, dwarfing as they do most of the older, more modest and less pretentious buildings. The neighborhoods outside the downtown area remain extant and intact, more or less, as they have always maintained themselves. Along with the Junior Museum, the eminence of Corona Heights, which figures so prominently in *The Pale Brown Thing*, still survives, and rises above the surrounding terrain. And still, despite all the new skyscrapers, the City has somehow—by some real miracle—retained much, if not most, of her old-time charm and fascination.

In a somewhat analogous way, *The Pale Brown Thing* has also retained its genuine and eerie enchantment, evoking as it does a rare and magical period in history that will never return, any more than will Fritz himself—alas! For those fortunate enough to have known him as a close friend, Fritz will always stand out as a rare and magical individual, and as I have maintained many times over the years, Fritz remains, through his multifarious writings, a great thinker, a great writer, a great mentor and—above all else—a prince among friends, a friend of friends.

Donald Sidney-Fryer
Auburn, California
12 October 2015

xiii

The Pale Brown Thing

The Pale Brown Thing

The solitary steep hill called Corona Heights was black as pitch and very silent, like the heart of the unknown. It looked steadily downward and away at the nervous bright lights of downtown, as if it were a great predatory beast of night surveying its territory in patient search of prey.

On every side of Corona Heights the street and house lights of San Francisco, weakest at end of night, hemmed it in apprehensively, as if it were indeed a dangerous animal. But on the hill itself there was not a single light.

Someday the hill might be bulldozed down, when greed had grown even greater than it is today and awe of primeval nature even less, but now it could still awaken panic terror.

Too savage and cantankerous for a park, it was inadequately designated as a playground. True, there were some tennis courts and limited fields of grass and low buildings and little stands of thick pine around its base, but above those it rose rough, naked, and contemptuously aloof.

And now something seemed to stir in the massed darkness there. Hard to tell what. Perhaps one or more of the city's wild dogs, homeless for generations. Perhaps some wilder and more secret animal that had never submitted to man's rule, yet lived almost unglimpsed amongst him. Perhaps, conceivably, a man (or woman) so sunk in savagery or psychosis that he (or she) didn't need light. Or perhaps only the wind.

And now the eastern horizon grew dark red, the whole sky lightened from the east toward the west, the stars were fading, and Corona Heights began to show its raw, dry, pale-brown surface.

Yet the impression lingered that the hill had grown restless, having at last decided on its victim.

Two hours later, Franz Westen looked out of his open casement window at the 1,200-foot TV tower rising bright red and white in the morning sunlight out of the snowy fog that still masked Sutro Crest and Twin Peaks three miles away (and against which Corona Heights stood out, humped and pale brown). It was his morning greeting to the universe, his affirmation that they were in touch, before making coffee and settling back into bed with clipboard and pad for the day's work of writing supernatural horror stories. A year or so ago—that was another matter.

Dancing up the sea air into his room, there came the gay sweet notes of a Telemann minuet blown by Cal from her recorder two floors below. She meant them for him, he told himself, even though he was twenty years older. He looked at the oil portrait of Daisy over the studio bed, beside a drawing of the TV tower in spidery black lines on a large oblong of fluorescent red cardboard, and felt no guilt. Three years of drunken grief—a record wake!—had worked that all away, ending almost exactly a year ago.

His gaze dropped to the studio bed, still half unmade. On the undisturbed half, nearest the wall, there stretched out a long colorful scatter of magazines, science-fiction paperbacks, a few hardcover detective novels still in their wrappers, and a half dozen of those shiny little *Golden Guides* and *Knowledge Through Color* books—his recreational reading as opposed to his working references arranged on the coffee table beside the bed. They'd been his chief, almost his sole companions during the three years he'd lain sodden there stupidly goggling at the TV across the room, but always fingering them and stupefiedly studying their bright easy pages from time to time. Only a month or so ago it had suddenly occurred to him that their gay casual scatter added up to a slender carefree woman lying beside him on top of the covers—that was why he never put them on the floor, why he contented himself with half the bed, why he unconsciously arranged them in a female form with long, long legs. They were a "scholar's mistress", he decided, on the analogy of "Dutch wife", that long slender bolster sleepers clutch to soak up sweat in tropical countries—a very secret playmate, a dashing but studious call girl, a slim incestuous sister, eternal comrade of his writing work.

With an affectionate glance toward his oil-painted dead wife and a keen warm thought toward Cal still sending up on the air pirouetting notes, he said softly with a conspiratorial smile to the slender cubist form occupying all the inside of the bed, "Don't worry, dear, you'll always be my best girl, though we'll have to keep it a deep secret from the others," and turned back to the window.

It was the TV tower standing way out there so modern tall on Sutro Crest, its three long legs still deep in fog, that had first got him hooked on reality again after his long escape in drunken dreams. At the beginning the tower had seemed unbelievably cheap and garish to him, an intrusion worse than the high rises in what had been the most romantic of cities. But then it had begun to impress him against his will with its winking red lights at night—so many of them! he had counted nineteen—and then it had subtly led his interest to the other distances in the cityscape and also in the real stars so far beyond and on lucky nights the moon, until he had got passionately interested in all real things again. And the process had never stopped, it still kept on.

Until Saul had said to him, "I don't know about welcoming in every new reality. You could run into a bad customer."

"That's fine talk, coming from a clinical psychologist," Gunnar had said, while Franz had responded instantly: "Taken for granted. Concentration camps. Germs of plague."

"I don't mean things like those exactly," Saul had said. "I guess I mean the sort of things some of my guys run into at the hospital."

"But those would be hallucinations, projections, archetypes, and so on, wouldn't they?" Franz had observed, a little wonderingly. "Parts of *inner* reality, of course."

"Sometimes I'm not so sure," Saul had said slowly. "Who's going to believe a crazy if he says he's just seen a ghost? Inner or outer reality? Who's to tell then? What do you say, Gunnar, when one of your computers starts giving read-outs it shouldn't?"

"That it's got overheated," Gun had answered with conviction. "Besides, my computers are normal people to start out with, not weirdos and psychotics like your guys."

Franz had smiled at his two friends; Cal had smiled too, though not so much.

Now he looked out the window again. Just outside it, the six-story drop went down past Cal's window—a narrow shaft between this building and the next, the flat roof of which was about level with his floor. Just beyond that, framing his view to either side, were the bone-white, rain-stained back walls, mostly windowless, of two high rises that went up and up.

It was a rather narrow slot between them, but through it he could see all of reality he needed to keep in touch. And if he wanted more he could always go up two stories to the roof, which he often did these days and nights.

From this building low on Nob Hill the sea of roofs went down and down, then up and up again, tinying with distance, to the bank of fog now masking the dark-green slope of Sutro Crest and the bottom of the tripod TV tower. But in the middle distance a shape like a crouching beast, pale brown in the morning sunlight, rose from the sea of roofs. The map called it just Corona Heights. It had been teasing Franz's curiosity for several weeks. Now he focused his small, seven-power Nikon binoculars on its bare earth slopes and humped spine, which stood out sharply against the white fog. Could it be called Corona Heights from the crown of irregularly clumped big rocks on its top? he asked himself as he rotated the knurled knob a little more, and they came out momentarily sharp and clear against the fog.

A rather thin, pale-brown rock detached itself from the others and waved at him. Damn the way these glasses jiggled with his heartbeat! A person who expected to see neat steady pictures through them just hadn't used binoculars. Or could it be a floater in his vision?—a microscopic speck in the eye's fluid? There he had it again! Just as he'd thought, it was some tall person in a long raincoat or drab robe moving about almost as if dancing. You couldn't see human figures in any detail at two miles even with sevenfold magnification; you just got a general impression of movements and attitude. They were simplified. This skinny figure on Corona Heights was moving around rather rapidly, all right, maybe dancing with arms waving high, but that was the most you could tell.

As he lowered the binoculars, he smiled broadly at the thought of some hippy type greeting the morning sun with ritual prancings on a mid-city hilltop newly emerged from fog. Someone from the Haight-Ashbury, likely, it was out that way. A stoned priest of a modern sun god dancing around his little accidental high-set Stonehenge. The thing had given him a start at first, but now he found it very amusing.

He set down the binoculars on his desk beside two old thin books. The topmost, bound in dirty gray, was open at its title page, which read in a utilitarian type face and layout marking it as last century's—a grimy job by a grimy printer with no thought of artistry: *Megapolisomancy: A New Science of Cities* by Thibaut de Castries. Now that was a funny coincidence! He wondered if a drug-crazed priest in earthen robes—or a dancing rock, for that matter!—would have been recognized by that strange old crackpot Thibaut as one of the "secret occurrences" he had predicted for big cities in the solemnly straight-faced book he'd written when he was relatively young in the 1890s. Franz told himself that he must read some more in it, and in the other book too.

But not right now, he told himself suddenly. He'd just remembered that today was a holiday for him (last night he'd sent two stories to his agent), and he was beginning to get an idea of what to do with it. He got dressed, made himself a cup of coffee, and carried it down to Cal's — and on an afterthought the two books under his arm and the binoculars in his coat pocket.

It was one of those times when Cal looked like a serious schoolgirl of seventeen, lightly wrapped in dreams, and not ten years older, her actual age. Long dark hair, blue eyes, a quiet smile. They'd been to bed together twice, but didn't kiss now—it might have seemed presumptuous on his part, she didn't quite offer to, and in any case he wasn't sure how far he wanted to commit himself. She invited him in to the breakfast she was making. Her room looked much nicer than his, too good for the building; she had redecorated it completely with help from Gunnar and Saul. Only it didn't have a view. There was a music stand by the window and an electronic piano that was mostly keyboard and black box and that had earphones for silent practicing, as well as a speaker.

They ate toast, juice and eggs. While she was pouring him more coffee, he said, "I've got a great idea. Let's go to Corona Heights today. I think there'd be a great view of downtown and the inner bay. We could take the Muni most of the way and there shouldn't be too much climbing."

"You forget I've got to practice for the concert tomorrow night and couldn't risk my hands in any case," she said a shade reproachfully. "But don't let that stop you," she added with a smile that asked his pardon. "Why not ask Gun or Saul, I think they're off today. Gun's great on climbing. Where is Corona Heights?"

He told her, remembering that her interest in Frisco was neither as new nor as passionate as his—he had a convert's zeal.

"That must be close to Buena Vista Park," she said. "Now don't go wandering in there, please. There've been some murders in there quite recently. Drug related. The other side of Buena Vista is right up against the Haight."

"I don't intend to," he said, "though maybe you're a little too uptight about the Haight. It's quieted down a lot the last few years. Why, I got these two books there in a really fabulous second-hand store."

"Oh, yes, you were going to show them to me," she said. He handed her the one that had been open, saying, "That's just about the most fascinating book of pseudo-science I've ever seen—it has some genuine insights mixed with the hokum. No date, but printed about 1900, I'd judge."

" 'Megapolisomancy'," she pronounced carefully. "Now what would that be? Telling the future from . . . from cities?"

"From *big* cities," he said, nodding.

"Oh, yes, the mega."

He went on: "Telling the future and all other sorts of things. And apparently making magic too from that knowledge. Though de Castries calls it 'a new science', as if he were a second Galileo. Anyhow, this de Castries is very much concerned about the 'vast amounts' of steel and paper that are being accumulated in big cities. And coal oil (kerosene) and natural gas. And electricity too, if you can believe it—he carefully figures out just how much electricity is in how many thousands of miles of wire, how many tons of illuminating gas in tanks, how much steel in the new skyscrapers, how much paper for government records and yellow journalism, and so on."

"My, oh, my," Cal commented. "I wonder what he'd think if he were alive today."

"His direst predictions vindicated no doubt. He *did* speculate about the growing menace of automobiles and gasoline, but especially electric cars carrying buckets of direct electricity around in batteries. He came so close to anticipating our modern concern about pollution—he even talks of 'the vast congeries of gigantic fuming vats' of sulfuric acid needed to manufacture steel. But what he was agitated about was the psychological or spiritual (he calls them 'paramental') effects of all that stuff accumulating in big cities, its sheer liquid and solid mass."

"A real proto-hippy," Cal put it. "What's with the other book?"

"Something quite interesting," Franz said, passing it over: "As you can see, it's not a regular book at all but a journal of blank rice-paper pages, as thin as onion skin but more opaque, bound in ribbed silk that was tea rose, I'd say, before it faded. The entries, in violet ink with a fine-point fountain pen, I'd guess, hardly go a quarter of the way through. The rest of the pages are blank. Now when I bought these books they were tied together with an old piece of string. They looked like they'd been joined for decades—you can still see the marks."

"Uh-huh," Cal agreed. "Since 1900 or so? A very charming diary book—I'd like to have one like it."

"Yes, isn't it? No, just since 1928. A couple of the entries are dated and they all seem to have been made in the space of a few weeks."

"Was he a poet?" Cal asked. "I see groups of indented lines. Who was he, anyway? Old de Castries?"

"No, not de Castries, though someone who had read his book and knew him. But I do think he was a poet. In fact, I think I have identified the writer, though it's not easy to prove since he nowhere signs himself. I think he was Clark Ashton Smith."

"I've heard that name," Cal said.

"Probably from me," Franz told her. "He was another supernatural horror writer. Very rich, doomful stuff: Arabian Nights chinoiserie. A mood like Beddoes' *Death's Jest-Book*. He lived near San Francisco and knew the old artistic crew; he visited George Sterling at Carmel, and he could easily have been here in San Francisco in 1928 when he'd just begun to write his finest stories. I've given a photocopy of that journal to Jaime Donaldus Byers, who's an authority on Smith and who lives here on Beaver Street (which is just by Corona Heights, by the way—the map shows it). Byers says there's no evidence for an extended San Francisco trip by Smith then and that although the writing looks like Smith's, it's more agitated than any he's ever seen. But I have reasons to think Smith would have kept the trip secret and have had cause to be supremely agitated."

"Oh, my," Cal said. "You've gone to a lot of trouble and thought about it. But I can see why. It's *très romantique*, just the feel of this ribbed silk and rice paper."

"I had a special reason," Franz said, unconsciously dropping his voice a little. "I bought the books four years ago, you see, before I moved here, and I read a lot of the journal. The violet-ink person (whoever, *I* think Smith) keeps writing about 'visiting Tiberius at 607 Rhodes'. In fact, the journal is entirely, or chiefly, an account of a series of such interviews. That '607 Rhodes' stuck in my mind, so that when I went hunting a cheaper place to live and was shown the room here—"

"Of course, it's your apartment number, 607," Cal interrupted.

Franz nodded. "I got the idea it was predestined, or prearranged in some mysterious way. As if I'd had to look for the '607 Rhodes' and had found it. I had a lot of mysterious drunken ideas in those days. In fact, I was pretty drunk most of the time, period."

"You certainly were," Cal agreed, "though in a quiet way. Saul and Gun and I wondered about you, and we pumped Dorotea Luque," she added, referring to the Peruvian apartment manager. "Even then, you didn't seem an ordinary lush. Dorotea said you wrote 'ficci*ón* to scare, about *espectros y fantasmas y los muertos y las muertas*,' but that she thought you were a gentleman."

Franz laughed. "Specters and phantoms of dead men and dead ladies. How very Spanish! Still, I'll bet you never thought—" he began and stopped.

"That I'd some day get into bed with you?" Cal finished for him. "Don't be too sure. I've always had erotic fantasies about older men. But tell me, how did your weird then-brain fit in the Rhodes part?"

"It never did," Franz confessed. "Though I still think the violet-ink person had some definite place in mind, besides the obvious reference to Tiberius's exile by Augustus to the island of Rhodes, where the Roman emperor-to-be studied oratory along with sexual perversion and a spot of witchcraft. The violet-ink person doesn't always say Tiberius, incidentally. It's sometimes Theobald and sometimes Tybalt, and once it's Thrasyllus, who was Tiberius's personal fortune-teller and sorcerer. But always there's that '607 Rhodes'. And once it's Theudebaldo and once Dietbold, but three times Thibaut, which is what makes me sure, besides all the other things, it must have been de Castries whom Smith was visiting almost every day and writing about."

"Franz," Cal said, "all this is perfectly fascinating, but I've just got to start practicing. Working up harpsichord on a dinky electronic piano is hard enough, and tomorrow night's not just anything, it's the Fifth Brandenburg Concerto."

"I know, I'm sorry I forgot about it. It was inconsiderate of me, a male chauvinist—" Franz began, getting to his feet.

"Now don't get tragic," Cal said briskly. "I enjoyed every minute, really, but now I've got to work. Here, take your cup and for heaven's sake these books, or I'll be peeking into them when I should be practicing. Cheer up—at least you're not a male chauvinist pig, you only ate one piece of toast.

"And, Franz," she called. He turned with his things at the door. "Do be careful up there around Beaver and Buena Vista. Take Gun or Saul. And remember—" Instead of saying what, she kissed two fingers and held them out toward him for a moment, looking quite solemnly into his eyes.

He smiled, nodded twice, and went out feeling happy and excited. He passed the elevator, although the cage was still there, and the strange black window beside it, and he climbed the red-carpeted stairs. He didn't stop at Gun and Saul's floor, however. He mightn't go to Corona Heights at all, but he wouldn't ask either of them to come with him—it was a question of courage, or at least independence.

He didn't stop at his own floor, either, but kept on toward the roof, glimpsing at each landing more of the strange black windows that couldn't be opened and a few black doors without knobs in the empty red-carpeted halls. It was odd how buildings had secret spaces in them that weren't really hidden but were never noticed, like the windows to the five air shafts which had been painted black at some time to hide their dinginess, and the doors to the disused broom closets, which had lost their function with the passing of cheap maid service. He doubted anyone in the building ever consciously saw them, except himself, newly aroused to reality by the tower and all.

He passed through the cubical room housing the elevator's motor and noisy, old-fashioned mechanical relays, and he stepped out onto the flat, rather low-walled roof, its tar-embedded gravel gritting faintly under his shoes. The cool breeze was welcome.

To the east and north bulked the huge downtown buildings and whatever secret spaces they contained, blocking off the Bay. How old Thibaut would have scowled at the Transamerica Pyramid and the purple-brown Bank of America monster! Even at the new Hilton and St. Francis towers. The words came into his head: "The ancient Egyptians only buried people in their pyramids. We are living in ours." Now where had he read that? Why, in *Megapolisomancy*, of course. How apt! And did the modern pyramids have in them secret markings foretelling the future and crypts for sorcery?

He walked past the low-walled openings of the narrow air shafts lined with gray sheet iron, to the back of the roof and looked up between the nearby high rises (modest compared with those downtown) at the TV tower and Corona Heights. The fog was gone, but the pale irregular hump of the latter still stood out sharply in the morning sunlight. He looked through his binoculars, not very hopefully, but—yes, by God!—there was that crazy drab worshipper, or what not, still busy with his ritual, or whatever. If these glasses would just settle down! Now the fellow had run to a slightly lower clump of rocks and seemed to be peering furtively over it. Franz followed the apparent direction of his gaze down the crest and almost immediately came to its probable object: two hikers trudging up. Because of their colorful shorts and shirts, it was easier to make them out. Yet despite their flamboyant garb they somehow struck Franz as more respectable characters than the lurker at the summit. He wondered what would happen when they met at the top. Would the robed hierophant try to convert them? Or solemnly warn them off? Or stop them like the Ancient Mariner and tell them an eerie story with a moral? Franz looked back, but now the fellow (or could it have been a woman?) was gone. A shy type, evidently. He searched the rocks, trying to spot him hiding, and even followed the plodding hikers until they reached the top and disappeared on the other side, hoping for a surprise encounter, but none came.

Nevertheless, when he shoved the binoculars back in his pocket, he had made up his mind. He'd visit Corona Heights. It was too good a day to stay indoors.

"If you won't come to me, then I will come to you," he said aloud, quoting an eerie bit from a Montague Rhodes James ghost story.

An hour afterwards he was climbing Beaver Street, taking deep breaths to avoid panting later. When he'd started, he'd had his binoculars hanging around his neck on their strap like a story-book adventurer's, so that Dorotea Luque, waiting in the lobby with a couple of elderly tenants for the mailman, had observed merrily, "You go to look for the e'scary thing to write e'stories about, no?" and he had replied, *"Si, Señora Luque. Espectros y fantasmas,"* in what he hoped was equally cock-eyed Spanish. But then a block or so back, a bit after getting off the Muni car on Market, he'd wedged them into his pocket again, alongside the street guide he'd brought. This seemed a nice-enough neighborhood, quite safe-looking, really. Still, there was no point in displaying advertisements of affluence. Actually there were relatively few people in the streets this morning. At the moment he couldn't see a single one. His mind toyed briefly with the notion of a big modern city suddenly completely deserted, like the barque the *Marie Celeste.*

He went by Jaime Donaldus Byers' place, a narrow-fronted piece of carpenter's Gothic now painted olive with gold trim, very Old San Francisco. Perhaps he'd chance ringing the bell coming back.

From here he couldn't see Corona Heights at all. Nearby stuff masked it (and the TV tower too). Conspicuous at a distance, it had hidden itself like a pale brown tiger on his approach, so that he had to get out his street guide and spread its map to make sure he hadn't got off the track.

At last he came out on a short dead-end cross street behind some new apartments. At its other end a sedan was parked with two people sitting in the front seats—then he saw that he'd mistaken headrests for heads. They did look so like dark little tombstones!

On the other side of the cross street were no more buildings, but green and brown terraces going up to an irregular crest against blue sky. He saw he'd finally reached Corona Heights, somewhat on the far side from his apartment.

After a leisurely cigarette, he mounted steadily past some tennis courts and up a winding hillside stairway and emerged on another dead-end street, or road, rather. He felt very good, really, in the outdoors. Gazing back the way he'd come, he saw the TV tower looking enormous (and handsomer than ever) less than a mile away, yet somehow just the right size. After a moment he realized that was because it was now the same size his binoculars magnified it to from his apartment.

Strolling to the dead end of the road, he passed a long, rambling one-story brick building with generous parking space that modestly identified itself as the Josephine Randall Junior Museum. There was a panel truck with the homely label *Sidewalk Astronomer*. He recalled hearing of it from Dorotea Luque's daughter Bonita as the place where children could bring pet tame squirrels and snakes and brindled Japanese rats (and bats?) when for some reason they could no longer keep them. He also realized he'd seen its low roofs from his window.

From the dead end, a short path led him to the foot of the crest, and there on the other side was all the eastern half of San Francisco and the Bay beyond and both the bridges spread out before him.

Resolutely resisting the urge to scan in detail, he set himself to mounting the ridge by the hard, gravelly path near its crest. This soon became rather tiresome. He had to pause more than once for breath and set his feet carefully to keep from slipping.

When he'd about reached the spot where he'd first seen the hikers, he suddenly realized that he'd grown rather childishly apprehensive. He was pausing now not so much for breath as to scan very carefully each rock clump before circling by it, for if he thrust his head too trustingly around one, what face or no-face might he not see?

This really was too childish of him, he told himself. Didn't he want to meet the character on the summit and find out just what sort of an oddball he was? A gentle soul, most likely, from his simple garb and timidity and love of solitude. Though of course he most likely had departed by now.

Nevertheless Franz kept using his eyes systematically as he mounted the last of the slope, gentler now, to its top.

The ultimate outcropping of rocks (the Corona?) was more extensive and higher than the others. After holding back a bit (to spy out the best route. he told himself) he mounted by three ledges, each of which required a leg-stretching step, to the very top, where he at last stood up with all of Corona Heights beneath him.

He slowly turned around in a full circle, tracing the horizon but scanning very thoroughly all the clumps of rock and all the brown and green slopes immediately below him, familiarizing himself with his new surroundings and incidentally ascertaining that there wasn't another being besides himself anywhere on Corona Heights.

Then he went down a couple of ledges and settled himself comfortably in a natural rock seat facing east. He felt very much at ease and remarkably secure in this eyrie, especially with the sense of the mighty TV tower rising behind him like a protective goddess. While smoking another leisurely cigarette, he surveyed with unaided eyes the great spread of the city and bay, with its great ships tinier than toys. It was interesting how landmarks shifted with his new vantage point. Compared with his view from the roof, some of the downtown buildings had shot up, while others seemed trying to hide behind their neighbors.

After another cigarette he got out his binoculars and put their strap around his neck and began to study this and that. They were quite steady now, not like this morning.

After a survey of the steely, gleaming inner waters and following the Bay Bridge all the way to Oakland, he set in seriously on the downtown buildings and soon discovered to his embarrassment that they were quite hard to identify from here. Distance and perspective had subtly altered their hues and arrangement. And, then, contemporary skyscrapers were so very anonymous—no signs or names, no pinnacle statues or weathercocks or crosses, no distinctive façades and cornices, no architectural ornament at all: just huge blank slabs of featureless stone, or concrete, or glass that was either sleekly bright with sun or dark with shadow. Really, they might well be the "gargantuan tombs or monstrous vertical coffins of living humanity, a breeding ground for the worst of paramental entities" that old de Castries had kept ranting about in his book.

After another stretch of telescopic study, in which he managed to identify a couple of the shifty skyscrapers at least, he let his binoculars hang and got out from his other pocket the meat sandwich he'd made himself. As he unwrapped and slowly ate it, he thought of what a fortunate person he really was. A year ago he'd been a mess, but now—

He heard a *scrutch* of gravel, then another. He looked around but didn't see anything. He couldn't decide from what direction the faint sounds had come. The sandwich was dry in his mouth.

With an effort he swallowed and continued eating and recaptured his train of thought. Yes, now he had friends like Gun and Saul . . . and Cal . . . and his health was a damn sight better

Another *scrutch*, louder, and with it an odd little high-pitched laugh. He tensed himself and looked around quickly, sandwich and thoughts forgotten. There came the laugh again, mounting toward a shrill shriek, and from behind the rocks there came dashing, along the path just below, two little girls in dark-blue play clothes. The one caught the other and they spun around, squealing happily, in a whirl of sun-browned limbs and fair hair.

Franz had barely time to think what a refutation this was of Cal's (and his own) worries about this area, and for the afterthought that still it didn't seem right for parents to let such small, attractive girls (they couldn't be more than seven or eight) ramble in such a lonely place, when there came loping from behind the rocks a shaggy St. Bernard, whom the girls at once pulled into their whirling game.

But after only a little more of that, they ran on along the path by which Franz had come up, their large protector close behind. He smiled. His sandwich no longer tasted dry.

He crumpled the wax paper into a ball and stuck it in his pocket. The sun was already westering and striking the distant tall walls confronting him. His trip and climb had taken longer than he'd realized, and he'd been sitting here longer too. What was that epitaph Dorothy Sayers had seen on an old tombstone and thought the acme of all grue? Oh, yes: "It is later than you think." They'd made a popular song of that just before World War II: "Enjoy yourself, enjoy yourself, it's later than you think." There was shivery irony for you! But he had lots of time.

He got busy with his binoculars again, studying the medieval greenish brown cap of the Mark Hopkins Hotel housing the restaurant-bar Top of the Mark. An obviously pleasant task occurred to him: to spot his own seven-story apartment house. From his window he could see Corona Heights. Ergo, from Corona Heights he could see his window. It would be in a narrow slot between two high rises, he reminded himself, but the sun would be striking into that slot by now, giving good illumination.

To his chagrin, it proved extremely difficult. From here the lesser roofs were almost a trackless sea, literally, and such a foreshortened one that it was very hard to trace the lines of streets—a checkerboard viewed from the edge. The job preoccupied him so that he became oblivious of his immediate surroundings. If the little girls had returned now and stared up at him, he probably wouldn't have noticed them. Yet the silly little problem he'd set himself was so puzzling that more than once he almost gave it up.

Really, a city's roofs were a whole dark alien world of their own, unsuspected by the myriad dwellers below, and with their own inhabitants, no doubt, their own ghosts and "paramental entities". But he rose to the challenge, and with the help of a couple of familiar water-tanks he knew to be on roofs close to his and of a sign Bedford Hotel painted in big black letters high on the side wall of that nearby building, he at last identified his apartment house. He was wholly engrossed in his task.

Yes, there was the slot, by God!—and there was his own window, the second from the top, very tiny but distinct in the sunlight. Lucky he'd spotted it now—the shadow travelling across the wall would soon obscure it.

And then his hands were suddenly shaking so that he'd dropped his binoculars. Only the strap kept them from crashing on the rocks.

A pale brown shape had leaned out of his window and waved at him.

What was going through his head was a couple of lines from that bit of silly folk doggerel which begins:

Taffy was a Welshman, Taffy was a thief.
Taffy came to my house and stole a piece of beef.

But it was the ending that was repeating itself in his head:

I went to Taffy's house, Taffy wasn't home.
Taffy went to my house and stole a marrow bone.

Now for God's sake don't get so excited, he told himself, taking hold of the dangling binoculars and raising them again. And stop breathing so hard, you haven't been running.

He was some time locating his building and the slot again—damn the dark sea of roofs!—but when he did, there was the shape again in his window. Pale brown, like old bones—now don't get morbid! It could be the drapes, he told himself, half blown out of his window by the wind—

he'd left it open. Among high buildings there were freakish winds. His drapes were green, of course, but their lining was a nondescript hue like this. And the figure wasn't waving to him now—its dancing was that of the binoculars—but rather regarding him thoughtfully, as if saying, "You chose to visit my place, Mr. Westen; so I decided to make use of that opportunity to have a quiet look at yours." Quit it! he told himself. The last thing we need now is a writer's imagination.

He lowered his binoculars to give his heartbeat a chance to settle down and to work his cramped fingers. Suddenly anger filled him. In his fantasizing he'd lost sight of the plain fact that someone was mucking about in his room! But who? Dorotea Luque had a master key, of course, but she was never a bit sneaky, nor her grave brother Fernando, who did the janitor work and had hardly any English at all but played a remarkably strong game of chess. Franz had given his own duplicate key to Gun a week ago—a matter of a parcel to be delivered while he was out—and hadn't got it back. Which meant that either Gun or Saul, or Cal for that matter, might have it now. Cal had a big old faded bathrobe she sometimes mucked around in—

But, no, it was ridiculous to suspect any of them. Face up to it, while he was gadding about out here, satisfying obscure esthetic curiosities, some sneak thief, probably on hard drugs, had somehow got into his apartment and was ripping him off.

He took up the binoculars again in a hard fury and found his apartment at once, but this time he was too late. While he'd been steadying his nerves and wildly speculating, the sun had moved on, the slot had filled with shadow, so that he could no longer make out his window, let along any figure in it.

His anger faded. He realized it had been mostly reaction to his little shock at what he'd seen, or thought he'd seen . . . no, he'd *seen* something, but as to exactly what, who could be sure?

He stood up on his rocky seat, rather slowly, for his legs were a bit numb from sitting and his back was stiff, and he stepped carefully up into the wind. He felt depressed—and no wonder, for streamers of fog were blowing in from the west, around the TV tower and half masking it, there were shadows everywhere. Corona Heights had lost its magic for him, he just wanted to get off it as soon as possible (and back to check his room). So after a quick look at his map, he headed straight down the far side, as the hikers had.

It was steeper than it looked, and several times he had to restrain his impulse to hurry and make himself move carefully. Then, halfway down, a couple of big dogs came to circle and snarl at him, not St. Bernards but those black Dobermans that always made one think of the SS. Their owner down below took his time calling them off, too. Franz almost ran across the green field at the hill's base and through the small door in the high wire fence.

Soon—but not too soon for him, by any means—he was hurrying along Buena Vista Drive East. The park it closely skirted—another elevation, but a wooded one—mounted up from beside him dark green and full of shadows. In his present mood it looked anything but a "good view" to him, rather an ideal spot for heroin intrigues and sordid murders. The sun was altogether gone by now and ragged arms of fog came curving after him. When he got to Duboce, he wanted to rush down, but the sidewalks were too steep—as steep as any he'd seen on any of San Francisco's more than seven hills—and once again he had to grit his teeth and place his feet with care and take his time.

He caught the N-Judah car where it comes out of the tunnel under Buena Vista Park (Frisco's hills were honeycombed with 'em, he thought) and rode it down Market to the Civic Center. Among the crowders boarding a 19-Polk there, a hulking drab shape lurching up behind him gave him a start, but it was only a blank-eyed workman powdered with pale dust from some demolition job.

He got off the 19 at Geary. In the lobby of 811 Geary there was only Fernando vacuuming, a sound as gray and hollow as the day had grown outside. He would have liked to chat, but the short man, blocky and somber as a Peruvian idol, had less English than his sister and was additionally rather deaf. They bowed gravely to each other, exchanged a "Senyor Lookay" and a "Meestair Jueston", Fernando's rendering of "Westen".

He rode the creaking elevator up to six. He had the impulse to stop at Cal's or the boys' first, but it was a matter of . . . well, courage, not to. The hall was dark (a ceiling globe was out) and the shaft window and knobless closet door next to his room darker. As he approached his own door, he realized his heart was thumping. Feeling both foolish and apprehensive, he slipped his key into the lock, and clutching his binoculars in his other hand as an impromptu weapon, he thrust the door swiftly open and quickly switched on the ceiling light inside.

The 200-watt glare showed his room empty and undisturbed. From the inside of the still-tousled bed, his colorful "scholar's mistress" seemed to wink at him humorously. Nevertheless, he didn't feel secure until he'd rather shamefacedly peered in the bathroom and then opened the closet and the tall clothes cabinet and glanced inside.

He switched off the top light then and went to the open window. The green drapes were lined with a sun-faded tan, all right, but if they'd been blown halfway out the window at some point, a change of wind had blown them neatly back into place afterwards. The serrated hump of Corona Heights showed up dimly through the advancing high fog.

The TV tower was wholly veiled. He looked down and saw that the window sill and his narrow desk abutting it and the carpet at his feet were all strewn with crumbles of brownish paper. He recalled that he'd been handling some old pulp magazines here yesterday, tearing out pages he wanted to save.

The tension that had been knotting him departed at last. He realized he was very thirsty. He got a split of ginger ale from the small refrigerator and drank it eagerly. While he made coffee on the hot plate, he sketchily straightened the disordered half of the bed and turned on the shaded light at its head. He carried there his coffee and the two books he'd shown Cal that morning, and settled himself comfortably, and read around in them and speculated.

When he realized it was getting darker outside, he poured himself more coffee and carried it down to Cal's. The door was ajar. Inside, Cal's shoulders were lifting rhythmically as she played with furious precision, her ears covered with large padded phones. Franz couldn't be sure whether he heard the ghost of a concerto or only the very faint thuds of the keys.

Saul and Gun were talking quietly on the couch, the latter with a green bottle beside him.

Saul, a thin man with dark hair shoulder-length and dark-circled eyes, quirked a smile and said, "Hello. Calvina asked us down to keep her company while she practices, though you'd think a couple of window dummies could do the job as well. But Calvina's a romantic puritan at heart. Deep inside she wants to frustrate us."

Cal had taken off her headphones and stood up. Without a word or a look at anyone, or anything apparently, she picked up some clothes and vanished like a sleepwalker into the bathroom, whence there came presently the sound of showering.

Gun grinned at Franz and said, "Greetings. Take a pew. How goes the writer's life?" He was a tall man, ashen blonde, a fine-down amiable Viking.

They talked inconsequentially and lazily of this and that. Saul carefully made a long thin cigarette. Its piny smoke was pleasant, but Franz and Gun smilingly declined to share, Gun tilting his green bottle for a long swallow.

Cal reappeared in a surprisingly short time, looking fresh and demure in a dark-brown dress. She poured herself a tall thin glass of orange juice from the fridge and sat down. "Saul," she said quietly, "you know my long name is not Calvina, but Calpurnia—the minor Roman Cassandra who kept warning Caesar. I may be a puritan, but I wasn't named for Calvin. My parents were both born Presbyterians, it's true, but my father early progressed into Unitarianism and died a devout Ethical Culturist. He used to pray to Emerson and swear by Robert Ingersoll. While my mother was, rather frivolously, into Bahai. And I don't own a couple of window dummies, or I might use them. No, no pot, thank you. I have to hold myself intact until tomorrow night. Franz, you look quietly prodigious. What happened at Corona Heights?"

Pleased that she had been thinking about him and observing him so closely and accurately, Franz told the story of his adventure. He was struck by how in the telling it became rather trivial seeming and less frightening, though paradoxically more entertaining—the writer's curse and blessing.

Gun happily summed up: "So you go to investigate this apparition or whatnot, and find it's pulled the big switch and is thumbing its nose at you from your own window two miles away. 'Taffy went to my house'— that's neat."

Saul said, "Your Taffy story reminds me of my Mr. Edwards. He gets the idea that two enemies in a parked car across the street from the hospital have got a pain-ray projector trained on him. We wheel him over there so he can see for himself there ain't no one in any of the cars. He's very much relieved and keeps thanking us, but when we get him back to his room, he lets out a sudden squeal of agony. Seems his enemies have taken advantage of his absence to plant a pain-ray projector somewhere in the walls."

Franz said; "Saul, I may very well have been projecting, at least in part, but, if so, what? Also, the figure was nondescript, remember, and wasn't doing anything objectively sinister."

Saul said, "Look, I wasn't suggesting any parallel. That's your idea. I was just reminded of another weird incident."

Gun guffawed. "Saul doesn't think we're all completely crazy. Just fringe-psychotic."

There was a knock and then the door opened as Dorotea Luque let herself in. She was a slender version of her brother, with a beautiful Incan profile and jet-black hair. She had a small parcel-post package of books for Franz.

"I wondered you'd be down here, and then I heard you talk," she explained. "Did you find the e'scary things to write about with your . . . how you say . . . ?" She made binoculars of her hands and held them to her eyes and then looked questioningly when they all laughed.

While Cal got her a glass of wine, Franz hastened to explain. To his surprise, she took the figure in the window very seriously.

"But are you e'sure you weren't ripped off?" she demanded anxiously. "We've had an e'stealer on the second floor."

"My portable TV and tape recorder were there," he told her. "A thief would take those first."

"But how about your marrow bone?" Saul put in. "Taffy get that?"

"And did you close your transom and double-lock your door?" Dorotea persisted, illustrating the latter with a vigorous twist of her wrist. "Is double-locked now?"

"I always double-lock it," Franz assured her. "The transom, no. I like it open for ventilation."

"Should always close the transom too when you go out," she pronounced. "All of you, you hear me? Well, I am glad you weren't ripped off. *Gracias*," she added, nodding to Cal as she sipped her wine.

Cal smiled and said to Saul and Gun, "Why shouldn't a modern city have its special ghosts, like castles and graveyards and big manor houses once had?"

Saul said, "My Mrs. Willis thinks the skyscrapers are out to get her. At night they make themselves still skinnier, she says, and come sneaking down the streets after her."

Gun said, "I once heard lightning whistle over Chicago. There was a thunderstorm over the Loop, and I was on the South Side at the university, right near the site of the first atomic pile. There'd be a flash on the northern horizon and then, seven seconds later, not thunder, but this high-pitched moaning scream. I had the idea that all the elevated tracks were audio-resonating a radio component of the flash."

Cal said eagerly, "Why mightn't the sheer mass of all that steel—? Franz, tell them about the book."

He repeated what he'd told her this morning about *Megapolisomancy* and a little besides.

Gun broke in, "And he says our modern cities are our Egyptian pyramids? That's beautiful. Just imagine how, when we've all been killed off by pollution, an archaeological expedition arrives by spaceship from another solar system and starts to explore us like a bunch of goddamn Egyptologists! What would they make of the World Trade Center in New York City and the Empire State? Or the Sears Building in Chicago? Or even the Transamerica Pyramid here? They'd probably decide they were all built for religious and occult purposes, like Stonehenge. They'd never imagine people lived and worked there. No question, our cities will be the eeriest ruins ever. Franz, this de Castries had a sound idea—the sheer amount of stuff there is in cities. That's heavy, heavy."

Saul put in: "Mrs. Willis says the skyscrapers get very heavy at night when they—excuse me—screw her."

Dorotea Luque's eyes grew larger, then she exploded in giggles. "Oh, that's naughty," she reproved him merrily, wagging a finger. Gun got her more wine and himself another bottle of ale.

Cal said, "Franz, I've been thinking on and off all day, in the corner of my mind that wasn't Brandenburging, about that '607 Rhodes' that drew you to move here. Was it a definite place? And if so, where?"

"607 Rhodes, what's that all about?" Saul asked. Franz explained again about the rice-paper journal and the violet-ink person who might have been Clark Ashton Smith and his possible interviews with de Castries. Then he said, "The 607 can't be a street address, like 811 Geary here, say. There's no such street as Rhodes in Frisco, I've checked. And it's clear from the entries that the 607 place is here downtown, within easy walking distance of Union Square. And once the journal keeper describes looking out the window at Corona Heights and Mt. Sutro—of course, there wasn't any TV tower then—

"Hell, in 1928 there weren't even the Bay and Golden Gate Bridges," Gun put in.

Cal said, "Maybe Rhodes is the name of a building or hotel. You know, the Rhodes Building."

"Not unless the name's been changed since 1928," Franz told her. "There's nothing like that now that I've heard of. The name Rhodes strike a bell with any of you?"

It didn't. Gun speculated, "I wonder if *this* building ever had a name, the poor old raddled dear."

Dorotea shook her head. "Is just 811 Geary. Was once hotel, maybe—you know, night clerk and maids. But I don't know."

"Buildings Anonymous," Saul remarked without looking up from the reefer he was making.

"Now we do close transom," said Dorotea, suiting actions to words. "Okay smoke pot. But do not—how you say?—advertise."

Heads nodded wisely.

After a bit they all decided that they were hungry and should eat together at the German Cook's around the corner because it was his night for sauerbraten. Dorotea was persuaded to join them. On the way she picked up her daughter Bonita and the taciturn Fernando, who now beamed.

Walking together, Cal asked Franz, "Taffy is something more serious than you're making out, isn't it?"

He had to agree, though he was becoming curiously uncertain of some of the things that had happened today—the usual, not-unpleasant evening fog settling around his mind. High in the sky, the lopsided circle of the gibbous moon challenged the streetlights.

He said, "When I thought I saw that thing in my window, I strained for all sorts of explanations, to avoid having to accept a . . . well, supernatural one. I even thought it might have been you in your old bathrobe."

"Well, it could have been me, except it wasn't," she said calmly. "I've still got your key, you know. Gun gave it to me that day your big package was coming and Dorotea was out. I'll give it to you after dinner."

"No hurry," he said.

"I wish we could figure out that 607 Rhodes," she said.

"I'll try to think of a way," he said. "Cal, did your father actually swear by Robert Ingersoll?"

"Oh, yes—'In the name of . . . ' and so on—and by William James, too, and Felix Adler, the man who founded Ethical Culture. His rather atheistic co-religionists thought it odd of him, but he liked the ring of sacerdotal language. He thought of science as a sacrament."

At the friendly little restaurant they put two tables together. Gun switched to a dark beer. Saul ordered a bottle of red wine for himself and the Luques. The sauerbraten was delicious, the potato pancakes with applesauce out of this world. Bela, the gleaming-faced German Cook (Hungarian, actually) had outdone himself.

In a lull in the conversation Gun said to Franz, "That was really a very strange thing that happened to you on Corona Heights. As near as you can get today to what you'd call the supernatural."

Saul heard and said at once, "Hey, what's a materialist scientist like you doing talking about the supernatural?"

"Come off it, Saul," Gun answered with a chuckle. "I deal with matter, sure. But what is that? Invisible particles, waves, and force fields. Nothing solid at all. Don't teach your grandmother to suck eggs."

"You're right," Saul grinned, sucking his. "There's no reality but the individual's immediate sensations, his awareness. All else is inference. Even the individuals are inference."

Cal said, "I think the only reality is number . . . and music, which comes to the same thing."

"My computers agree with you, all the way down the line," Gun told her. "Number is all they know."

Franz said, "I'm glad to hear you all talk that way. You see, supernatural horror is my bread and butter, and sometimes people tell me there's no such thing any more—that science has solved, or can solve, all mysteries, that religion is just another name for social service, and that modern people are too sophisticated and knowledgeable to be scared of ghosts even for kicks."

"Don't make me laugh," Gun said. "Science has only increased the area of the unknown. And if there is a god, her name is Mystery."

Dorotea Luque said eagerly, "But are e-strange things. In Lima. This city too. *Brujas*—how you say?—witches!" She shuddered happily.

Her brother beamed his understanding and lifted a hand to preface one of his rare remarks. "*Hay hechicería*." he said vehemently, with a great air of making himself clear, "*Hechicería ocultada en murallas*." He crouched a little, looking up. "*Murallas muy altas!*"

Everyone nodded pleasantly, as if they understood. Franz asked Cal in a low voice, "What's that?"

She whispered, "Witchcraft, I think. Witchcraft hidden in the wall. Very high walls." She shrugged.

Franz murmured, "Where in the walls, I wonder? Like Mr. Edwards' pain-ray projector?"

Gun said, "There's one thing, though, Franz, I do wonder about—whether you really identified your own window correctly from Corona. You said the roofs were like a sea on edge. It reminds me of difficulties I've run into in identifying localities in photographs of stars, or pictures of the earth taken from satellites. So many times you run into two or more localities that are *almost* identical."

"I've thought of that myself," Franz said. "I'll check it out." Leaning back, Saul said, "Say, here's a good idea, let's all of us some day soon go for a picnic to Corona Heights. Gun and I could bring our ladies—they'd like it. How does that grab you, Bonny?"

"Oh, yes," the thirteen-year-old Bonita, already as tall as her mother, replied eagerly.

On that note they broke up.

Dorotea said, "We thank you for the wine. But all remember, double-lock doors and close transoms when go out."

Cal said, "Now with any luck I'll sleep twelve hours. Franz, I'll give you your key some other time."

He smiled and asked Fernando if he cared to play chess. The Peruvian grinned agreeably.

In Franz's room they divided two rather long, hard-fought games, which were just the thing to occupy fully Franz's dulled evening mind, and during them he became aware of how physically tired his climbing had left him.

As Fernando departed, the Peruvian pointed at the board and asked, "*Mañana por la noche?*"

That much Spanish Franz understood. He smiled and nodded. If he couldn't play chess again tomorrow night, he could always let Dorotea know.

He slept like the dead and without any remembered dreams.

He awoke completely refreshed, his mind clear and sharp and very calm, his thoughts measured and sure—a good sleep's benison. All of the evening dullness and uncertainty were gone. He remembered each of yesterday's events just as it had happened, but without the emotional overtones of excitement and fear.

The constellation of Orion was shouldering into his window, telling him dawn was near. Its nine brightest stars made an angular, tilted hourglass, challenging the smaller, slenderer one made by the nineteen winking red lights of the TV tower.

He made himself a small, quick cup of coffee with the very hot water from the tap, then put on slippers and robe and took up his binoculars and went very quietly to the roof. All his sensations were sharp. The black windows of the shafts and the black knobless doors of the disused closets stood out as distinctly as the doors of the occupied rooms and the one banister, many times repainted, he touched as he climbed.

In the room on the roof his small flashlight showed the gleaming cables, the dark, hunched electric motor, and the oddly bunched small, silent iron arms of the relays that would wake violently and make a great sudden noise, swinging and snapping, if someone pressed an electric button below.

Outside, the night wind was bracing.

He looked up at the stars studding the dark dome of night like tiny silver nails. Bringing his binoculars into play, he scanned the golden swarm of the Hyades and the tiny bluish-white dipper of the Pleiades.

The sure and steady stars fitted the mood of his morning mind and reinforced it. He looked again at tilted Orion, then dropped his gaze to the red-flashing TV tower. Below it, Corona Heights was a black hump amongst the city's lights.

The memory came to him (crystal-clear drop, as memories came to him these days in the hour after waking) of how when he'd first seen the TV tower at night, he'd thought of a line from Lovecraft's story, "The Haunter of the Dark", where the watcher of another ill-omened hill (Federal in Providence) sees that "the red Industrial Trust beacon had blazed up to make the night grotesque." When he'd first seen the tower, he'd thought it worse than grotesque, but now—how strange!—it had become almost as reassuring to him as starry Orion.

"The Haunter of the Dark!" he thought with a quiet laugh. Yesterday he had lived through a section of a story that might fittingly be called "The Lurker at the Summit". How very strange!

Before returning to his room he briefly surveyed the dark rectangles and skinny pyramid of the downtown sky-scrapers—old Thibaut's bugaboos!—the tallest of them with their own warning red lights.

He made himself more coffee, this time using the hot plate and adding sugar and half-and-half. Then he settled himself in bed, determined to use his morning mind to clarify matters that had grown cloudy last evening. Thibaut's drab book and the washed out tea-rose journal already made the head of his colorful Scholar's Mistress lying beside him on the inside. To them he added the thick black rectangles of Lovecraft's *The Outsider* and *The Collected Ghost Stories* of Montague Rhodes James and also several yellowed old copies of *Weird Tales* (some puritan had torn their lurid covers off) containing stories by Clark Ashton Smith, shifting some bright magazines to the floor to make room, and the colorful napkins with them.

"You're fading, dear," he told her gaily in his thoughts, "putting on somber hues. Are you getting dressed for a funeral?"

Then for a space he read more systematically in *Megapolisomancy*. My God, the old boy certainly could do a sort of scholarly-flamboyant thing quite well. Consider:

At any particular time of history there have always been one or two cities of the monstrous sort—*viz.*, Babel or Babylon, Ur-Lhassa, Ninevah, Syracuse, Rome, Samarkand, Tenochtitlan, Peking—but we live in the Megapolitan (or Necropolitan) Age, when such disastrous blights are manifold and threaten to conjoin and enshroud the world with funebral yet multipotent city-stuff. We need a Black Pythagoras to spy out the evil lay of our monstrous cities and their foul shrieking songs, even as the White Pythagoras spied out the lay of the heavenly spheres and their crystalline symphonies, two and a half millennia ago.

Or, adding thereto more of his own brand of the occult:

Since we modern city-men already dwell in tombs, inured after a fashion to mortality, the possibility arises of the indefinite prolongation of this life-in-death. Yet, although quite practicable, it would be a most morbid and dejected existence, without vitality or even thought, but only paramentation, our chief companions paramental entities of azoic origin more vicious than spiders or weasels.

Now what would paramentation be like? Franz wondered. Trance? Opium dreams? Dark, writhing phantoms born of sensory deprivation? Or something different?

Or:

> The electro-mephitic city-stuff whereof I speak has potencies for achieving vast effects at distant times and localities, even in the far future and on other orbs, but of the manipulations required for the production and control of such I do not intend to discourse in these pages.

As the overworked, yet vigorous current exclamation had it, *wow*! Franz picked up the journal.

Smith (he was sure it was he) had certainly been greatly impressed by de Castries (must be he also), as well he might have been almost fifty years ago. And he had clearly read *Megapolisomancy* too. It occurred to Franz that this copy was most likely Smith's. Here was a typical passage in the journal:

> Three hours today at 607 Rhodes with the furious Tybalt. All I could take. Half the time railing at his fallen-off acolytes, the other half contemptuously tossing me scraps of paranatural truth. But what scraps! That bit about the significance of diagonal streets! How that old devil sees into cities and their invisible sicknesses—a new Pasteur, but of the dead-alive.

He says his book is kindergarten stuff, but the new thing—the core and why of it and how to work it—he keeps only in his mind and in the Grand Cipher he's so sly about, sometimes calls it (the Cipher) his Fifty-Book, that is, if I'm right and they are the same. Why fifty?

I should write Howard about it, he'd be astounded and—yes!—transfigured, it so agrees with *and illuminates* the decadent and putrescent horror he finds in New York City and Boston and even Providence (not Levantines and Mediterraneans, but half-sensed paramentals!). But I'm not sure he could take it. For that matter, I'm not sure how much more of it I can take myself. And if I so much as hint to old Tiberius at sharing his paranatural knowledge with other kindred spirits, he grows as ugly as his namesake in his last Caprian days and goes back to excoriating those whom he feels failed and betrayed him in the Hermetic Order he created.

I should get out myself—I've all that I can use and there are stories crying to be written. But can I give up the ultimate ecstasy of knowing each day I'll hear from the very lips of Black Pythagoras some new paranatural truth? It's like a drug I have to have. Who can give up such fantasy?—especially when *the fantasy is the truth.*

The paranatural, only a word—*but what it signifies!* The supernatural—a dream of grandmothers and priests and horror writers. But the *paranatural!* Yet how much can I take? Could I stand full contact with a paramental entity and not crack up?

Coming back today, I felt that my senses were metamorphosing. San Francisco was a mega-necropolis vibrant with paramentals on the verge of vision and of audition, each block a surreal cenotaph would bury Dali, and I one of the living dead aware of everything with cold delight. But now I am afraid of this room's walls!

Franz glanced with a chuckle at the drab wall next to the inside of the bed and below the spiderwebby drawing of the TV tower on fluorescent red, remarking to his Scholar's Mistress lying between them, "He certainly was worked up about it, wasn't he, dear?"

Then his face grew intent again. The "Howard" in the entry had to be Lovecraft, with his regrettable but undeniable loathing of the immigrant swarms he felt were threatening the traditions and monuments of his beloved New England and the whole Eastern Seaboard. While the mention of a Black Pythagoras was pretty well enough by itself to prove that the keeper of the journal had read de Castries' book. And those references to a Hermetic Order and a Grand Cipher (or Fifty-Book) teased the imagination. But Smith (who else?) had clearly been as much terrified as fascinated by the ramblings of his crabbed mentor. It showed up even more strikingly in a later entry:

Hated what gloating Tiberius hinted today about the disappearance of Bierce and the deaths of Sterling and Jack London. Not only that they were suicides (which I categorically deny, particularly in the case of Sterling!) but that there were other elements in their deaths—elements for which the old devil appears *to take credit.*

He positively sniggered as he said, "You can be sure of one thing, my dear boy, that all of them had a very rough time *paramentally* before they were snuffed out, or shuffled off to their gray paranatural hells. Very distressing, but it's the common fate of Judases—and little busybodies," he added, glaring at me from under his tangled white eyebrows.

Could he be hypnotizing me?

Why do I linger on, now that the menaces outweigh the revelations? That disjointed stuff about techniques of giving paramental entities the scent—clearly a threat.

Franz frowned. He knew quite a bit about the brilliant literary group centered in San Francisco at the turn of the century and of the strangely large number of them who had come to tragic ends,—among those, the macabre writer Ambrose Bierce vanishing in revolution-torn Mexico in 1913, London dying of uremia and morphine poisoning a little later, and the fantasy poet Sterling perishing of poison in the 1920s. He reminded himself to ask Jaime Donaldus Byers more about the whole business at the first opportunity.

The final diary entry, which broke off in the middle of a sentence, was the same vein:

Today surprised Tiberius making entries in black ink in a ledger of the sort used for bookkeeping. His Fifty-Book? The Grand Cipher? I glimpsed a solid page of what looked like astronomical and astrological symbols (Could there be fifty such?) before he snapped it shut and accused me of spying. I tried to get him off the topic, but he would talk of nothing else.

Why do I stay? The man is a genius (paragenius?) but he's also a paranoiac!

He shook the ledger at me, cackling, "Perhaps you should sneak in some night on those quiet little feet of yours and steal it! Yes, why not do that? It would merely mean your finish, paramentally speaking! That wouldn't hurt. Or would it?" Yes, by God, it is time I—

Franz riffled through the next few pages, all blank, and then gazed over them at the window, which from the bed showed only the equally blank wall of the nearer of the two high rises. It occurred to him what an eerie fantasia of *buildings* all this was: de Castries' ominous theories about them, Smith seeing San Francisco as a . . . yes, mega-necropolis, Lovecraft's horror of the swarming towers of New York, the downtown skyscrapers seen from the roof here, the sea of roofs he'd scanned from Corona Heights, and this beaten old building itself, with its dark halls and yawning lobby, strange shafts and closets, black windows and hiding holes.

He made himself more coffee—it had been full daylight now for some time—and lugged back to bed with him an armful of books from the shelves of his desk. To make room for them, more of the colorful recreational reading had to go on the floor. He joked with his Scholar's Mistress, "You're growing darker and more intellectual, my dear, but not a day older and as slim as ever. How do you manage it?"

The new books were a fair sampling of what he thought of as his reference library of the really eerie. There was Prof. D. M. Nostig's *The Subliminal Occult*, that curious, intensely skeptical book which rigorously disposes of all claims of the learned parapsychologists and still finds a residue of the inexplicable; Montague's witty and profound monograph *White Tape* with its thesis that civilization is being asphyxiated, mummy-wrapped by its own records, bureaucratic and otherwise, and by its infinitely recessive self-observations; precious dingy copies of those two exceedingly rare, slim books thought spurious by many critics—*Ames et Fantômes de Douleur* by the Marquis de

Sade and *Knockenmädchen im Pelze mit Peitsche* by Sacher-Masoch; *The Mauritzius Case* by Jacob Wasserman; *Journey to the End of Night* by Céline; several copies of Bonewitz's periodical *Gnostica*; *The Spider Glyph in Time* by Mauricio Santos-Lobos; and the monumental *Sex, Death and Supernatural Dread* by Ms. Frances D. Lettland, Ph.B.

For a long space his morning mind darted about happily in the eerie wonder-world evoked and buttressed by these books and de Castries' and the journal and by clear-cut memories of yesterday's rather strange experiences. Truly, modern cities were the world's supreme mysteries, and skyscrapers their secular cathedrals.

Meanwhile his intentions were firming as to how he'd spend this day, which promised to be a beauty too. First, start pinning down that elusive 607 Rhodes, beginning by getting the history of this anonymous building, 811 Geary. It would make an excellent test case. Next go to Corona Heights again to check out whether he'd really seen his own window from there. Sometime in the afternoon visit Jaime Donaldus Byers. (Call him first.) Tonight, of course, Cal's concert.

He blinked and looked around. Despite the open window, the room was full of smoke. With a sorry laugh he carefully stubbed out his cigarette on the edge of the heaped ashtray.

The phone rang. It was Cal inviting him down to late breakfast. He showered and shaved and dressed and went.

In the doorway Cal looked so sweet and young in a green dress, her hair in a long pony tail, that he wanted to grab and kiss her. But she also still had on her rapt, meditative look—"Keep intact for Bach."

She said, "Hello, dear. I actually slept those twelve hours I threatened to in my pride. God is merciful. Do you mind eggs again? It's really brunch-time. Pour yourself coffee."

"Any more practice today?" he asked, glancing toward the electronic keyboard.

"Yes, but not with that. This afternoon I'll have three or four hours with the concert harpsichord. And I'll be tuning it."

He drank creamed coffee and watched the poetry of motion as she dreamily broke eggs, an unconscious ballet of white ovoids and slender, work-flattened fingertips. He found himself comparing her to Daisy and, to his amusement, to his Scholar's Mistress. Cal and the latter were both slender, somewhat intellectual, rather silent types, touched with the White Goddess definitely, dreamy but disciplined. Daisy had been touched with the White Goddess too, a poet, and also disciplined, keeping herself intact . . . for brain cancer. He veered off from that.

Cal really did look such a schoolgirl, her face a mask of gay innocence and good behavior. But then he remembered her as she had launched into the first piece of a concert. He'd been sitting up close and a little to one side so that he had seen her full profile. As if by some swift magic, she had become someone he'd never seen before and wasn't sure for a moment he wanted to. Her chin had tucked down into her neck, her nostril had flared, her eye had become all-seeing and merciless, her lips had pressed together and turned down at the corners quite nastily, like a savage schoolmistress, and it had been as if she had been saying, "Now hear me, all you strings and *Mister* Chopin. You behave perfectly now, *or else* . . . !" It had been the look of the young professional.

"Eat them while they're hot," Cal murmured, slipping his plate in front of him. "Here's the toast. Buttered, somehow."

After a while she asked, "How did you sleep?"

He told her about the stars.

She said, "I'm glad you worship."

"Yes, that's true in a way," he had to admit. "Saint Copernicus, at any rate, and Isaac Newton."

"My father used to swear by them too," she told him. "Even, I remember once, by Einstein. I started to do it myself too, but mother gently discouraged me. She thought it tomboyish."

Franz smiled. He didn't bring up this morning's reading or yesterday's events, they seemed wrong topics for now.

She observed placidly, "You're very brisk and brimming with energy this morning. Almost bumptious, except you're being considerate for my mood. But underneath you're thoughtful. What are your plans for today?"

He told her.

"That sounds good," she said. "I've heard Byer's place is quite spooky. Or maybe they meant exotic. And I'd really like to find out about 607 Rhodes. That would be fascinating. Well, I should be getting ready."

"Will I see you before? Take you there?" he asked as he got up.

"No, not before, I think," she said thoughtfully. "But afterwards." She smiled at him. "I'm relieved to hear you'll be there. Take care, Franz."

"You take care too, Cal," he told her.

"On concert days I wrap myself in wool. No, wait." She came toward him, head lifted, continuing to smile. He got his arms around her before they kissed. Her lips were soft and cool.

An hour later a pleasantly grave young man in the recorder's office at city hall informed Franz that 811 Geary Street was designated Block 320, Lot 23 in his province.

"For anything about the lot's previous history," he said, "you'd go to the assessor's office. They would know, because they handle taxes."

Franz crossed the wide, echoing marble corridor two stories high to the assessor's office, which flanked the main entrance to city hall on the other side. The two great civic guards and idols, he thought, papers and monies.

A worried woman with graying red hair told him, "Your next step is to go to the office of building permits in the city hall annex across the street, to your left when you go out, and find when a permit to build on the lot was applied for. When you bring us that information, we can help you. It should be easy. They won't have to go back far. Everything in that area went down in 1906."

Franz obeyed, thinking that all this was becoming not just a fantasia but a ballet of buildings. Investigating just one modest building had led him into what you could call this Courtly Minuet of the Run-Around. Doubtless the bothersome public was supposed to get bored and give up at this point, but he'd fool 'em! The brimming spirits Cal had noticed in himself were still high.

Yes, a national ballet of all buildings great and small, skyscrapers and shacks, all going up and haunting our streets and cross streets for a while and then eventually coming down, whether helped by earthquakes or not, to the tune of ownership, money, and records.

In the annex, a business-like building with low ceilings, Franz was pleasantly surprised (but his cynicism rather dashed) when a portly young Chinaperson, upon being properly supplicated with the ritual formula of numbered block and lot, within two minutes handed him a folded old printed form filled in with ink that had turned brown and which began "Application for Permit to erect a seven-story Brick Building with Steel Frame on the south side of Geary Street twenty-five feet west of Hyde Street at Estimated Cost of $74,870.00 for Use as a Hotel," and ended with "Filed July 15, 1925".

His first thought was that Cal and the others would be relieved to hear that the building apparently had a steel frame—a point they'd wondered about during earthquake speculations and to which they'd never been able to get a satisfactory answer. His second was that the date made the building almost disappointingly recent—the San Francisco of Dashiell Hammett . . . and Clark Ashton Smith. Still, the big bridges hadn't been built then, ferries did all their work. Fifty years was a respectable age.

He copied out most of the brown-ink stuff, returned the application to the stout young man (who smiled, hardly inscrutably) and footed it back to the assessor's office, swinging his briefcase jauntily. The red-haired woman was worrying elsewhere, and two ancient men who both limped received his information dubiously, but finally deigned to consult a computer, joking together as to whether it would work, but clearly reverent for all their humor.

One of them pushed some buttons and read off from a screen invisible to the public, "Yep, permit granted September 9, 1925, and built in '26. Construction completed Jun—June."

"They said it was for use as a hotel," Franz asked. "Could you tell me what name?"

"For that you'd have to consult a city directory for the year. Ours don't go back that far. Try in the public library across the square."

Franz dutifully crossed the wide gray expanse, dark green with little segregated trees and bright with small gushing fountains and two long pools rippling in the wind. On all four sides the civic buildings stood pompously, most of them blocky nondescript, but city hall behind him with its greenish dome and classic cupola and the main public library ahead somewhat more decorated.

Feeling ebullient and now a bit lucky too, Franz hurried. He still had much to do today and the high sun said it was getting on. Inside the swinging doors he angled through the press of harsh young women with glasses, children, belted hippies, and cranky old men (typical readers all), returned two books, and took the elevator to the empty corridor of the third floor. In the hushed, rather elegant San Francisco Room a slightly precious lady whispered to him that her city directories only went up to 1918, the later (more common?) ones were in the main catalogue room on the second floor with the phone books.

Feeling slightly deflated and a bit run-around again, but not much, Franz descended to the big, fantastically high-ceilinged familiar room. In a corner partitioned off by high, packed shelves, he found the rows of books he wanted. His hand went toward the 1926, then shifted to the 1927—that would be sure to list the hotel, if there had been one. Now for some fun!—looking up the addresses of everyone mentioned in the application and finding the hotel itself, of course.

Before seating himself he glanced at his wristwatch. My God, it was later than he'd thought. If he didn't make up some time, he'd arrive at Corona Heights after the sun had left the slot and so too late for the experiment he intended. And books like this didn't circulate.

He took only a couple of seconds coming to a decision. After a casual but searching look all around to make sure no one was watching him at the moment, he thrust the directory into his deep brief case and marched out of the catalogue room, picking up a couple of paperbacks at random from one of the revolving wire stands set here and there. He stopped at the desk to check them out and drop them ostentatiously into his brief case, and then walked out of the building without a glance at the guard, who never did look into brief cases and bags (so far as Franz had noticed) provided he'd seen you check out some books at the desk.

Franz seldom did that sort of thing, but today's promise seemed to make it worth taking little risks.

There was a 19-Polk coming outside. He caught it.

At 811 he glanced at his mail (nothing worth opening right away) and then looked around the room. He'd left the transom open. Dorotea was right—a thin, athletic person could crawl through it. He shut it. Then he leaned out the open casement window and checked each way—to either side and up (one window like his, then the roof) and down (Cal's two below and, three below that, the shaft's grimy bottom, a cul-de-sac, scattered with junk fallen over the years). There was no way anyone could reach this window short of using ladders. But he noticed that his bathroom window was only a short step away from the window of the next apartment on this floor. He went and made sure it was locked.

Then he took off the wall the big spidery black sketch of the TV tower that was almost entirely bright fluorescent red background and securely wedged and thumbtacked it, red side out, in the open casement window, using drawing pins. There! That would show up unmistakably from Corona in the sunlight when it came.

Next he put on a light sweater under his coat (it seemed a bit chillier than yesterday) and stuck an extra pack of cigarettes in his pocket. He didn't pause to make himself a sandwich (after all, he'd had *two* pieces of toast this morning at Cal's). At the last minute he remembered to stuff his binoculars and map into his pocket, *and* Smith's journal; he might want to refer to it at Byers' (He'd called the man up earlier and got a typically effusive but somewhat listless invitation to drop in any time after the middle of the afternoon and stay if he liked for the little party coming up in the evening. Some of the guests would be in costume, but costume was not mandatory.)

As a final touch he placed the 1927 city directory where his Scholar's Mistress' rump would be and, giving it a quick intimate caress, said flippantly, "There, my dear, I've made you a receiver of stolen property, but don't worry, you're going to give it back."

Then without further leave-taking, or any send-off at all, he double-locked the door behind him and was away into the wind and sunlight.

At the corner there was no bus coming, and so he started to walk the eight short blocks to Market, striding briskly. At Ellis he deliberately devoted a few seconds to looking at (worshipping?) his favorite tree in San Francisco: a six-story candlestick pine, guyed by some thin strong wires, greenly flourishing behind a brown wooden wall trimmed with yellow between two taller buildings in a narrow notch the high-rise moguls had somehow overlooked. Inefficient bastards!

A block farther on, the bus overtook him and he got aboard—it would save a minute. Transferring to the N-Judah car at Market, he got a start (and had to side-step swiftly) when a pallid drunk in a shapeless, dirty, pale-gray suit (but no shirt) came staggering diagonally from nowhere (and apparently bound for the same place). He thought, "There but for the grace of God, et cetera," and veered off from those thoughts, as he had at Cal's from the memories of Daisy's mortal disease.

In fact, he banished all dark stuff so well from his mind that the creaking car seemed to mount Market and then Duboce in the bright sunlight like the victorious general's chariot in a Roman triumph. He swung off at the tunnel's mouth and climbed dizzying Duboce, breathing deeply. It seemed not quite so steep today, or else he was fresher. While the neighborhood looked particularly neat and friendly.

At the top a young couple hand in hand (lovers quite obviously) were entering the dappling shades and green glooms of Buena Vista Park. Why had the place seemed so sinister yesterday? Some other day he'd follow in their path to the park's pleasantly wooded summit.

But today his was another voyage—he had other business. Pressing business, too. He glanced at his wristwatch and stepped along smartly. Soon he was going through the little gate in the high wire fence and across the green field back of the brown-sloped heights with their rocky crown. To his right, two little girls were supervising a sort of dolls' tea party on the grass. Why, they were the girls he'd seen running yesterday. And just beyond them their St. Bernard was stretched out beside a young woman in faded blue denim.

While to the left, two Dobermans—the same two, by God!—were stretched out and yawning beside another young couple lying close together though not embracing. As Franz smiled at them, the man smiled back and waved a casual greeting. It really was that poet's cliché, "an idyllic scene".

He would have lingered, but time was wasting. Got to go to Taffy's house, he thought with a chuckle. He mounted the ragged, gravelly slope—it wasn't all that steep!—with just one breather. Over his shoulder the TV tower stood tall, her colors bright, as fresh and gussied-up and elegant as a brand new whore. (Your pardon, Goddess.) He felt fey.

When he got to the corona, he noticed something he hadn't yesterday. Several of the rock surfaces, at least on this side, had been scrawled on at past times with dark and pale and various colored paints from spray cans, most of it rather weathered now. There weren't so many names and dates as simple figures. Lopsided five and six-pointed stars, a sunburst, crescents, triangles, and squares. He thought of—of all the things!—de Castries' Grand Cipher. Yes, he noted with a grin, there were symbols here that could be taken as astronom- and/or -logical. Those circles with crosses and arrows—Venus and Mars. While that horned disk might be Taurus.

You certainly have odd tastes in interior decoration, Taffy, he told himself. Now to check if you're stealing my marrow bone.

Well, spray-painting signs on rocky eminences was standard practice these progressive, youth-oriented days—the graffiti of the heights. Though he recalled how at the beginning of the century the black magician Aleister Crowley had spent a summer painting in huge red capitals on the Hudson palisades DO WHAT THOU WILT IS THE ONLY COMMANDMENT and EVERY MAN AND WOMAN IS A STAR to shock and instruct New Yorkers on the river boats.

He found his stone seat of yesterday and then made himself smoke a cigarette to give himself time to steady his nerves and breathing, and relax, although he was impatient to make sure he'd kept ahead of the sun. Actually he knew he had, though by a rather slender margin. His wristwatch assured him of that.

It was clearer and sunnier than yesterday, if anything. The strong west wind was sweeping the air. The distant little peaks beyond the East Bay cities and north in Marin County stood out quite sharply. The bridges were bright. Even the sea of roofs itself seemed friendly and calm today.

With unaided eyes he located what he thought was the slot in which his window was—it was full of sun at any rate—and then got out his binoculars. He didn't bother to string them around his neck—his grip was firm today. Yes, there was the fluorescent red, all right, seeming to fill the whole window, the scarlet stood out so, but then you could tell it just occupied the lower left-hand quarter. Why, he could almost make out the drawing . . . no, that would be too much, those thin black lines.

So much for Gun's (and his own) doubts as to whether he'd located the right window yesterday!

But the seeing was certainly exceptionally fine today. How clearly pale yellow Coit Tower on Telegraph Hill, once Frisco's tallest structure, now a trifle, stood out against the blue bay. And the high rounded windows of the ship-shaped old Hobart Building's stern, that was like the lofty, richly encrusted admiral's cabin of a galleon, against the stark, vertical aluminum lines of the new Wells Fargo Building towering over it like a space to space interstellar freighter waiting to blast. He roved the binoculars around, effortlessly refining the focus.

He took another look into his window slot before the shadow swallowed it. Perhaps he could see the drawing if he 'fined the focus . . .

Even as he watched, the oblong of fluorescent cardboard was jerked out of sight. From his window there thrust itself a pale thing that wildly waved its long uplifted arms at him. While low between them he could see its face stretched toward him, a mask as narrow as a ferret's, a pale brown, utterly blank triangle, two points above that might mean eyes or ears, and one ending below in a tapered chin . . . no, snout . . . no, very short trunk—*a questioning mouth that looked as if it were for sucking marrow. Then the paramental entity reached through the glasses at his eyes.*

In his next instant of awareness he was hearing a hollow chunk and a faint tinkling and he was searching the dark sea of roofs with his naked eyes to try to locate anywhere a swift pale brown thing stalking him across them and taking advantage of every bit of cover: a chimney and its cap, a cupola, a water tank, a penthouse large or tiny, a thick standpipe, a wind scoop, a ventilator hood, hood of a garbage chute, a skylight, a roof's low walls, the low walls of an air shaft. His heart was pounding and his breathing fast.

His frantic thoughts took another turn, and he was scanning the slopes before and beside him, and the cover their rocks and dry bushes afforded. Who knew how fast a paramental travelled? as a cheetah? as sound? as light? It could well be back here on the heights already. He saw his binoculars below the rock against which he'd unintentionally hurled them when he'd thrust out his hands convulsively to keep the thing out of his eyes.

He scrambled to the top. From the green field below the little girls were gone, and their chaperon and the other couple and the three animals. But even as he was noticing that, a large dog (one of the Dobermans? or something else?) loped across it toward him and disappeared behind a clump of rocks at the base of the slope. He'd thought of running down that way, but not if that dog (and what others? and what else?) were on the prowl. There was too much cover on this side of Corona Heights.

He stepped quickly down and stood on his stone seat and made himself hold still and look out squintingly until he found the slot where his window was. It was full of darkness, so that even with his binoculars he wouldn't have been able to see anything.

He dropped down to the path, taking advantage of handholds, and while shooting rapid looks around, picked up his broken binoculars and jammed them in his pocket, though he didn't like the way the loose glass in them tinkled a little—or the gravel grated under his careful feet, for that matter. Such small sounds could give away a person's whereabouts.

One instant of awareness couldn't change your life this much, could it? But it had.

He tried to straighten out his reality, while not letting down his guard. To begin with, there were no such things as paramental entities, they were just part of de Castries' 1890s pseudo-science. But he had *seen* one, and as Saul had said, there was no reality except an individual's immediate sensations—vision, hearing, pain, those were real. Deny your mind, deny your sensations, and you deny reality. Even to try to rationalize was to deny. But of course there were *false* sensations, optical and other illusions . . . Really, now!—try telling a tiger springing upon you he's an illusion. Which left exactly hallucination and, to be sure, insanity. Parts of inner reality . . . and who was to say how far inner reality went? As Saul had also said, "Who's going to believe a crazy if he says he's just seen a ghost? Inner or outer reality? Who's to tell then?" In any case, Franz told himself, he must keep firmly in mind that he might now be crazy—without letting down his guard one bit on that account either!

All the while that he was thinking these thoughts, he was moving watchfully, carefully, and yet quite rapidly down the slope, keeping a little off the gravel path so as to make less noise, ready to leap aside if something rushed him. He kept darting glances to either side and over his shoulder, noting points of concealment and the distances to them. He got the impression that something of considerable size was following him, something that was wonderfully clever in making its swift moves from one bit of cover to the next, something of which he saw (or thought he saw) only the edges. One of the dogs? Or more than one? Perhaps urged by rapt-faced, fleet-footed little girls. Or . . . ? He found himself picturing the dogs as spiders as furry and as big. Once in bed, her limbs and breasts pale in the dawn's first light, Cal had told him a dream in which two big borzoi following her had changed into two equally large and elegant creamy-furred spiders.

What if there were an earthquake now (he must be ready for *anything*), and the brown ground opened in smoking cracks and swallowed his pursuers up? And himself too?

He reached the foot of the crest and soon was circling past the Josephine Randall Junior Museum. His sense of being pursued grew less, or rather of being pursued at such close distance. It was good to be close to human habitations again, even if seemingly empty ones, and even though buildings were objects that things could hide behind. This was the place where they taught the boys and girls not to be afraid of rats and bats and giant tarantulas and other entities. Where were the children anyhow? Had some wise Pied Piper led them all away from this menaced locality? Or had they piled into the "Sidewalk Astronomer" panel truck and taken off for other stars? What with earthquakes and eruptions of large pale spiders and less wholesome entities, San Francisco was no longer very safe. Oh, you fool, watch, watch!

As he left the low building behind him and descended the hillside stairway and went past the tennis courts and finally reached the short dead-end cross street that was the boundary of Corona Heights, his nerves quieted down somewhat and his whirling thoughts too, though he got a dreadful start when he heard from somewhere a sharp squeal of rubber on asphalt and thought for a moment that the parked car at the other end of the cross street had started for him, steered by its two little tombstone headrests.

As he descended Beaver Street he began to encounter people at last, not many but a few. He remembered as if from another lifetime his intention to visit Byers (he'd even phoned) and debated whether to go through with it. He'd never been here before; his previous meetings in San Francisco with the man had been at a mutual friend's apartment in the Haight.

His mind was made up for him when an ambulance on Castro, which he'd just crossed, let loose with its yelping siren on approaching Beaver, and the foul, nerve-twanging sound growing suddenly unendurably loud as the vehicle crossed Beaver, fairly catapulted Franz up the steps to the faintly gold-arabesqued olive door and set him pounding the bronze knocker that was in the shape of a merman.

After a maddeningly long pause the polished brass knob turned, the door began to open, and a voice as grandiloquent as that of Vincent Price at his fruitiest said, "Here's a knocking indeed. Why, it's Franz Westen. Come in, come in. But you look shaken, my dear Franz, as if that ambulance had delivered you. What have the wicked, unpredictable streets done now?"

As soon as Franz was reasonably sure that the neatly bearded, rather theatric visage was Byers', he pressed past him, saying, "Shut the door. I *am* shaken," while he scanned the richly furnished entry and the large glamorous room opening from it and the thickly carpeted stairs ahead going up to a landing mellow with light that had come through stained glass and the dark hall beyond the stairs.

Behind him, Byers was saying, "All in good time. There, it's locked, and I've even thrown a bolt, if that makes you feel better. And now some wine? Fortified, your condition would seem to call for. But tell me at once if I should call a doctor, so we won't have that fretting us."

They were facing each other now. Jaime Donaldus Byers was about Franz's age, somewhere in the mid-forties, medium tall, with the easy, proud carriage of an actor. He wore a pale green Nehru jacket faintly embroidered in gold, similar trousers, leather sandals, and a long, pale-violet dressing gown, open but belted with a narrow sash. His well-combed auburn hair hung to his shoulders. His

Vandyke beard and narrow mustache were neatly trimmed. His palely sallow complexion, noble brow, and large liquid eyes were Elizabethan, suggesting Edmund Spenser. And he was fairly clearly aware of all this.

Franz, whose attention was still chiefly elsewhere, said, "No, no doctor. And no alcohol, this time, Donaldus. But if I could have some coffee, black . . . "

"My dear Franz, at once. Just come with me into the living room. Everything's there. But what is it that has shaken you? What's *chasing* you?"

"I am afraid," Franz said curtly and then added quickly, "of paramentals."

"Oh, is that what they're calling the big menace these days?" Byers said lightly, but his eyes had narrowed sharply first. "I'd thought it was the Mafia. Or the CIA. And there's Russia. I am only up to date sporadically. I live firmly in the world of art, where reality and fantasy are one."

And he motioned Franz to select a seat, while he busied himself at a heavy table on which stood slender bottles and two small steaming urns.

The room was furnished sybaritically, and while not specifically Arabian, there was much more ornamentation than depiction. Franz chose a large hassock that was set against a wall and from which he had an easy view of the hall, the rear archway, and the windows, whose faintly glittering curtains transmitted yellowed sunlight and blurred, dully gilded pictures of the outdoors. Silver gleamed from two black shelves beside the hassock, and Franz's gaze was briefly held against his will (his fear) by a collection of small statuettes of modish young persons engaged with great hauteur in various sexual activities, chiefly perverse—the style between Art Deco and Pompeian. Under any other circumstances he would have given them more than a passing scrutiny. They looked incredibly detailed and devilishly expensive. Byers, he knew, came of a wealthy family and produced a sizable volume of exquisite poetry and prose sketches every three or four years.

Now that fortunate person set a thin, large white cup half filled with steaming coffee and also a steaming silver pot upon a firm low stand by Franz that additionally held an obsidian ashtray. Then he settled himself in a convenient low chair, sipped the pale yellow wine he'd brought, and said, "You said you had some questions when you phoned. About that journal you attribute to Smith?—and of which you sent me a photocopy."

Franz answered, his gaze still roving systematically. "That's right. I do have some questions for you. But first I've got to tell you what happened to me just now."

"Of course. By all means. I'm most eager to know."

Franz tried to condense his narrative, but soon found he couldn't do much of that without losing significance and ended by giving a quite full and chronological account of the events of the past thirty hours. As a result, and with some help from the coffee, which he'd needed, and from his cigarettes, which he'd forgotten to smoke for nearly an hour, he began after a while to feel a considerable catharsis, and his nerves settled down a great deal. He didn't find himself changing his mind about what had happened or its vital importance, but having a sympathetic listener certainly did make a great difference emotionally.

For Byers paid close attention, helping him on by little nods and eye-narrowings and pursings of lips and voiced brief agreements and comments—at least they were mostly brief. True, those last weren't so much practical as esthetic. even a shade frivolous, but that didn't bother Franz at all, at first—he was so intent on his story—while Byers, even when frivolous, seemed deeply impressed and far more than politely credulous about all Franz told him.

When Franz briefly mentioned the bureaucratic run-around he'd got, Byers caught the humor at once, putting in, "Dance of the clerks, how quaint!" And when he heard about Cal's musical accomplishments, he observed, "Franz, you have a sure taste in girls. A harpsichordist! What could be more perfect? My current dear friend-secretary-playfellow-co-housekeeper-cum-moon-goddess is North Chinese, supremely erudite, and works in precious metals—she did those deliciously vile silvers, cast by the lost-wax process of Cellini. She'd have served you your coffee except it's one of our personal days, when we recreate ourselves apart. I call her Fa Lo Suee (the daughter of Fu Manchu—it's one of our semi-private jokes) because she gives the delightfully sinister impression of being able to make over the world if ever she chose. You'll meet her if you stay this evening. Excuse me, please go on." And when Franz mentioned the astrological graffiti on Corona Heights, he whistled softly and said, "How *very* appropriate!" with such emphasis that Franz asked him, "Why?" but he responded, "Nothing. I mean the sheer range of our tireless defacers. Next: a pyramid of beer cans on Shasta's mystic top. Pray, continue."

But when Franz mentioned *Megapolisomancy* a third or fourth time and even quoted from it, Byers lifted a hand in interruption and went to a tall bookcase and unlocked it and took from behind the darkly clouded glass a thin book bound in black leather beautifully tooled with silver arabesques and handed it to Franz, who opened it.

It was a copy of de Castries' gracelessly printed book, identical with his own copy, as far as he could tell, save for the binding. He looked up questioningly.

Byers explained, "Until this afternoon I never dreamed you owned a copy, my dear Franz. You only showed me the violet-ink journal, you'll recall, that evening in the Haight, and later sent me a photocopy of the written-on pages. You never mentioned buying another book along with it. And on that evening you were, well . . . rather tiddly."

"In those days I was drunk all of the time," Franz said flatly.

"I understand . . . poor Daisy . . . say no more. The point is this: *Megapolisomancy* happens to be not only a rare book but also, literally, a very secret one. In his last years, de Castries had a change of mind about it and tried to hunt down every single copy and burn them all. And did!—almost. He was known to have behaved vindictively toward persons who refused to yield up their copies. He was, in fact, a very nasty and, I would say (except I abhor moral judgments), evil old man. At any rate, I saw no point at the time in telling you that I possessed what I thought then to be the sole surviving copy of the book."

Franz said, "Thank God! I was hoping you knew something about de Castries."

Byers said, "I know quite a bit. But first, finish your story. You were on Corona Heights, today's visit, and had just looked through your binoculars at the Transamerica Pyramid, which made you quote de Castries on 'our modern pyramids . . . ' "

"I will," Franz said, and did it quite quickly, but it was the worst part. It brought vividly back to him his sight of the triangular pale brown muzzle and his flight down Corona Heights, and by the time he was done he was sweating and darting his glance about again.

Byers let out a sigh, then said with relish, "And so you came to me, pursued by paramentals to the very door!" And he turned in his chair to look somewhat dubiously at the blurry golden windows behind him.

"Donaldus!" Franz said angrily, "I'm telling you things that happened, not some damn weird tale I've made up for your entertainment. I know it all hangs on a figure I saw several times at a distance of two miles with seven power binoculars, and so anyone's free to talk about optical illusions and instrumental defects and the power of suggestion, but I know something about psychology and optics, and it was none of those!"

He finished icily, "Of course, it's quite possible I've gone insane, temporarily or permanently, and am 'seeing things', but until I'm sure of that I'm not going to behave like a reckless idiot—or a hilarious one."

Donaldus, who had been making protesting and imploring faces at him all the while, now said injuredly and placatingly, "My *dear* Franz, I never for a moment doubted your seriousness or had the faintest suspicion that you were psychotic. Why, I've been inclined to believe in paramental entities ever since I read de Castries' book, and especially after hearing several circumstantial, very peculiar stories about him; and now your truly shocking eye-witness narrative has swept my last doubts away. But I've not seen one yet—if I did, I'm sure I'd feel all the terror you do and more—but until then, and perhaps in any case, and despite the proper horror they evoke in us, they are most *fascinating* entities, don't you agree? Now as for thinking your account a tale or story, my dear Franz, to be a good story is to me the highest test of the truth of anything. I make no distinction whatever between reality and fantasy, or the objective and the subjective. All life and all awareness are ultimately one, including intensest pain and death itself. Not all the play need please us, and ends are never comforting. Some things fit together harmoniously and beautifully and startlingly with thrilling discords—those are true—and some do not, and those are merely bad art. Don't you see?"

Franz had no immediate comment. He certainly hadn't given de Castries' book the least credence by itself, but . . . he nodded thoughtfully, though hardly in answer to the question. He wished for the sharp minds of Gun and Saul.

"And now to tell you *my* story," the other said, quite satisfied. "But first a touch of brandy—that seems called for. And you? Well, some hot coffee then, I'll fetch it. And a few biscuits? Yes."

Franz had begun to feel headachy and slightly nauseated. The plain arrowroot cookies, barely sweet, seemed to help. He poured himself coffee from the fresh pot, adding some of the cream and sugar his host had thoughtfully brought this time.

Donaldus said, "You have to keep in mind de Castries died when I (and you) were infants. Almost all my information comes from a couple of the not-so-close and hardly well-beloved friends of de Castries' last declining years, George Ricker, who was a lock smith and played *go* with him, and Herman Klaas, who ran a second-hand bookstore on Turk Street and was a sort of romantic anarchist and for a while a Technocrat. And a bit from Clark Ashton Smith. Ah, that interests you, doesn't it? It was only a bit—Clark didn't like to talk about de Castries. I think it was because of de Castries and his theories that Clark stayed away from big cities, even San Francisco, and became the hermit of Auburn and Pacific Grove. And I've got some data from old letters and clippings, but not much. People didn't like to write down things about de Castries, and they had reasons, and in the end the man himself made secrecy a way of life.

"Also," Donaldus continued, "I'll probably tell the story, at least in spots, in a somewhat poetic style. Don't let that put you off. It merely helps me organize my thoughts and select the significant items. I won't be straying in the least from the strict truth as I've discovered it. Though there may be traces of paramentals in my story, I suppose, and certainly one ghost. I think all modern cities, especially the crass, newly built, highly industrial ones, should have ghosts. They are a civilizing influence."

He took a generous sip of brandy, rolled it around his tongue appreciatively, and settled back in his chair.

"In 1900, as the century turned," he began dramatically, "Thibaut de Castries came to sunny, lusty San Francisco like a dark portent from realms of cold and coal smoke in the East that pulsed with Edison's electricity and from which thrust Sullivan's steel framed skyscrapers. Madame Curie had just proclaimed radioactivity to the world, and Marconi radio spanning the seas. Madam Blavatsky had brought eerie theosophy from the Himalayas and passed on the occult torch to Annie Besant. The Scotch Astronomer-Royal Piazzi Smyth had discovered the history of the world and of its ominous future in the Grand Gallery of the Great Pyramid of Egypt. While in the law courts, Mary Baker Eddy and her chief female acolytes were hurling at each other accusations of witchcraft and black magic. Spencer preached science. Ingersoll thundered against superstition. Freud and Jung were plunging into the limitless dark of the subconscious. Wonders undreamed had been unveiled at the Universal Exhibition in Paris and at the World's Columbian Exposition in Chicago. New York was digging her subways. Count von Zeppelin was launching his first dirigible airship, while the Wright brothers were readying for their first flight.

"De Castries brought with him only a large black Gladstone bag stuffed with copies of his ill-printed book that he could no more sell than Melville his *Moby-Dick*, and a skull teeming with galvanic, darkly illuminating ideas, and (some insist) a large black panther on a leash of German silver links. He was a wiry, tireless, rather small black eagle of a man, with piercing eyes and sardonic mouth, who wore his glamor like an opera cape.

"There were a dozen legends on his origins. Some said he improvised a new one each night and some that they were all invented by others solely on the inspiration of his darkly magnetic appearance. The one that Klaas and Ricker most favored was moderately spectacular: that as a boy of thirteen during the Franco-Prussian war he had escaped from beseiged Paris by balloon along with his mortally wounded father, who was an explorer of darkest Africa, his father's beautiful and learned young Polish mistress, and a black panther (an earlier one) which his father had originally captured in the Congo and which they had just rescued from the zoological gardens, where the starving Parisians were slaughtering the wild animals for food. (Of course, another legend had it that at that time he was a boy aide-de-camp to Garibaldi in Sicily and his father the most darkly feared of the Carbonari.) The balloon landing in the Egyptian desert near Cairo, he plunged at once into a study of the Great Pyramid, assisted by his father's Polish mistress (now his own) and by the fact that he was maternally descended from Champollion, decipherer of the Rosetta Stone. He made all Piazzi Smyth's discoveries (and a few more besides, which he kept secret) ten years in advance and laid the basis for his new science of supercities (and also his Grand Cipher) before leaving Egypt to investigate mega-structures and cryptoglyphics (he called it) and paramentality throughout the world.

"You know, that link with Egypt fascinates me," Byers said parenthetically as he poured himself more brandy. "It makes me think of Lovecraft's Nyarlathotep, who came out of Egypt to deliver pseudo-scientific lectures heralding the crumbling away of the world.

"At all events, de Castries had acquired a lot of dark, satanic charm from somewhere by the time he arrived at the City by the Golden Gate. He *was*, I'd guess, quite a bit like the Satanist Anton La Vey (who kept a more-or-less tame lion for a while, did you know?) except that he had no desire for publicity. He was looking, rather, for an elite of scintillating, freethinking folk with a zest for life at its wildest—and if they had a lot of money, that wouldn't hurt a bit.

"And of course he found them!—the cream of the New World's freewheeling imaginative talent. Promethean (and Dionysian) Jack London. George Sterling, fantasy poet and romantic idol, favorite of the wealthy Bohemian Club set. Their friend, the brilliant defense attorney Earl Rogers, who later defended Clarence Darrow and saved his career. Ambrose Bierce, a bitter, becaped old eagle of a man himself, with his *Devil's Dictionary* and matchlessly terse horror tales. The poetess Nora May French. That mountain lioness of a woman, Charmion London. And those were only the more vitalic ones.

"And of course they fell upon de Castries with delight. He was just the sort of human curiosity they (and especially Jack London) loved. Mysterious cosmopolitan background, Munchausen anecdotes, weird and alarming scientific theories, a strong anti-industrial and (we'd say) anti-Establishment bias, the apocalyptic touch, the note of doom, hints of dark powers—he had them all! For quite a while he was their darling, their favorite guru of the left-handed path, almost (and I imagine he thought this himself) their new God. They even bought copies of his book and sat still (and drank) while he read from it. Prize egotists like Bierce put up with him, and London let him have stage center for a while—he could afford to. And they were all quite ready to go along (in theory) with his dream of a utopia in which megapolitan buildings were forbidden (had been destroyed or somehow tamed) and paramentally put to benign use, with themselves the aristocratic elite and he the master spirit over all.

"The high point came when with much hush-hush and weedings out and secret messages and some rare private occult pomps and ceremonies, I suppose, he organized the Hermetic Order—"

"Is that the Hermetic Order that Smith, or the journal, mentions?" Franz interrupted. He had been listening with a mixture of fascination, irritation, and wry amusement, with at least half his attention clearly elsewhere, but he had grown more attentive at mention of the Grand Cipher.

"It is," Byers nodded. "I'll explain. In England at that time there was a Hermetic Order of the Golden Dawn, an occult society with members like the mystic poet Yeats, who talked with vegetables and bees and lakes, and Dion Fortune and George Russell—A.E.—and your beloved Arthur Machen."

Franz nodded impatiently, restraining his impulse to say "Get on with it, Donaldus!"

The other got the point. "Well, anyhow," he continued, "In 1898 Aleister Crowley managed to join the Gilded Dayspringers (nice, eh?) and almost broke up the society by his demands for Satanistic rituals, black magic, and other real tough stuff.

"In imitation, but also as a sardonic challenge, de Castries called his society the Hermetic Order of the Onyx Dusk. He is said to have worn a large black ring of *pietra dura* work with a bezel of mosaicked onyx, obsidian, ebony, and black opal polished flat, depicting a predatory black bird, perhaps a raven.

"It was at this point that things began to go wrong for de Castries and that the atmosphere became, by degrees, very nasty.

"As nearly as I can reconstruct it, this is what happened. As soon as his secret society had been constituted, Thibaut revealed to its handful of highly select members that his utopia was not a far-off dream, but an immediate prospect, and that it was to be achieved by violent revolution, both material and spiritual (that is, paramental), and that the chief and at first sole instrument of that revolution was to be the Hermetic Order of the Onyx Dusk.

"This violent revolution was to begin with acts of terrorism somewhat resembling those the Nihilists were carrying out in Russia at that time (just before the abortive Revolution of 1905), but with a lot of new sort of black magic (his megapolisomancy) thrown in. Demoralization rather than slaughter was to be the aim, at least at first. Black-powder bombs were to be set off in public places and on the roofs of big buildings during the deserted hours of the night. Other big buildings were to be plunged into darkness by locating and throwing their main switches. Anonymous letters and phone calls would heighten the hysteria.

"But more important would be the megapolisomantic operations, which would cause 'buildings to crumple to rubble, people to go screaming mad, until every last soul is in panic flight from San Francisco, choking the roads and foundering the ferries'—at least that's what Klaas said de Castries confided to him many years later while in a rare communicative mood.

"These magical or pseudo-scientific acts (what would you call them?) would require absolute obedience on the part of Thibaut's assistants—which was the next demand Thibaut seems to have made of every last one of his acolytes in the Hermetic Order of the Onyx Dusk. One of them would be ordered to go to a specific address in San Francisco at a specified time and simply stand there for two hours, blanking his (or her) mind, or else trying to hold one thought. Or he'd be directed to take a bar of copper or a small box of coal or a toy balloon filled with hydrogen to a certain floor of a certain big building and simply leave it there (the balloon against the ceiling), again at a specified time. Apparently the elements were supposed to act as catalysts. Or two of three of them would be commanded to meet in a certain hotel lobby or at a certain park bench and just sit there together without speaking for half an hour. And everyone would be expected to obey every order unquestioningly and unhesitatingly, in exact detail, or else there would be (I suppose) various chilling Carboniar-style penalties and reprisals.

"Thibaut seems to have thought that there was, or that he had invented, a kind of mathematics whereby minds and big buildings (and paramental entities?) could be manipulated. Neopythagorean metageometry, he called it. It was all a question of knowing the right times and *spots* (he'd quote Archimedes' 'Give me a place to stand and I will move the world') and then conveying there the right person (and mind) or material object. Once, he started to outline in detail to Klaas a single act of megapolisomancy—give him the formula for it, so to speak—but then he got suspicious.

"Well, you can imagine how those prima donnas that he'd recruited reacted to all this. Conceivably Jack London and George Sterling might have gone through with things like the light-switch business for a lark, if they'd been drunk enough when Thibaut asked them. And even crochety old Bierce might have enjoyed a little mysterious black-powder thunder, if someone else did all the work and set it off. But when he asked them to do *boring* things he wouldn't explain, it was much too much. A dashing and eccentric society lady who was a great beauty (and an acolyte) is supposed to have said, 'If only he'd asked me to do something *challenging*, such as appear naked in the rotunda of the City of Paris and then swim out to Seal Rocks and chain myself to them like Andromeda. But just to stand in front of the public library thinking of the South Pole and saying nothing for an hour and twenty minutes—I *ask* you, darling!'

"When it got down to cases, you see, they must simply have refused to take him seriously, either his revolution or his new black magic.

"At any rate, they all refused to help him make even a test-run of his mega-magic. Or perhaps a few of them went along with it once or twice and nothing happened.

"I suppose that at this point he lost his temper and began to thunder orders and invoke penalties. And they just laughed at him—and when he wouldn't see that the game was over and kept up with it, simply walked away from him.

"Or took more active measures. I can imagine someone like London simply picking up the furious, spluttering little man by his coat collar and the seat of his pants and pitching him out.

"Something like that could have completed the transformation of Thibaut de Castries from a fascinating freak whom one humored into an unpleasant old bore, trouble maker, borrower, *and blackmailer*, against whom one protected oneself by whatever measures were necessary. Yes, Franz, there's the persistent rumor that he tried to and in some cases did blackmail his former disciples by threatening to reveal scandals he had learned about in the days when they were free with each other, or simply that they had been members of a terrorist organization—his own! Twice at this time he seems to have disappeared completely for several months, very likely because he was serving jail sentences—something several of his ex-acolytes were powerful enough to have managed easily, though I've never been able to track down an instance, so many records were destroyed in the Quake.

"But some of the old dark glamor must have lingered about him for quite a while in the eyes of his ex-acolytes— the feeling that he was a being with sinister, para-natural powers—for when the Earthquake did come very early in the morning of April 18th, 1906, thundering up Market in brick and concrete waves from the west and killing its hundreds, one of his lapsed acolytes, probably recalling his intimations of a magic that would topple skyscrapers, is supposed to have said, 'He's done it! The old devil's *done it!*'

"But mostly my information for this period is very sketchy and one-sided. The people who'd known him best were all trying to forget him (suppress him, you might say), while my two chief informants, Klaas and Ricker, knew him only as an old man in the 1920s and had heard only his side (or sides!) of the story. They both indignantly rejected the blackmail stories and the even nastier rumors that came later on: that de Castries was devoting his declining years to getting revenge on his betrayers by somehow doing them to death or suicide by black magic."

"I know about some of them," Franz said. "What happened to Nora May French?"

"She was the first to go. In 1907. A clear case of suicide."

"And when did Sterling die?"

"November 17th, 1926."

Franz said thoughtfully, though still not lost in thought, "There certainly seems to have been a suicidal drive at work, though operating over a period of twenty years. A good case can be made out that it was a death wish that drove Bierce to go to Mexico when he did—a war-haunted life, so why not such a death?—and probably attach himself to Pancho Villa's rebels as a sort of unofficial revolution-correspondent and most likely get himself shot as an uppity old gringo who wouldn't stay silent for the devil himself. While Sterling was known to have carried a vial of cyanide in his vest pocket for years, whether he finally took it by accident (pretty far-fetched) or by intention. And then there was that time (Rogers' daughter tells about it in her book) when Jack London disappeared on a five-day spree and then came home where Charmion and Rogers' daughter and several other worried people were gathered and with the mischievous, icy logic of a man who'd drunk himself sober, he challenged George Sterling and Earl Rogers to agree *not to sit up with the corpse.* Though I'd think alcohol was enough villain there, without bringing in any of de Castries' black magic, or its power of suggestion."

"What'd London mean by that?" Byers asked, squinting as he carefully measured out for himself more brandy.

"That when they felt life losing its zest, their powers starting to fail, they take the Noseless One by the arm without waiting to be asked, and exit laughing."

"The Noseless One?"

"Why, simply, London's sobriquet for Death himself—the skull beneath the skin. The nose is all cartilage and so the skull—"

Byers' eyes widened and he shot a finger toward his guest.

"Franz!" he asked excitedly, "That paramental you saw—wasn't it noseless?"

As if he'd just received a post-hypnotic command, Franz's eyes shut tight, he jerked back his face a little, and started to throw up his hands in front of it. Byers' words had brought the pale-brown, blank, triangular face vividly back to his mind's eye.

"Don't," he said carefully, "say things like that again without warning. Yes, it was noseless."

"My dear Franz, I will not. Please excuse me. I did not fully realize until now what effect the sight of it must have upon a person."

"All right, all right," Franz said quietly. "So four acolytes died somewhat ahead of their times (except perhaps for Bierce), victims of their rampant psyches . . . or of something else."

"And at least an equal number of the less prominent acolytes," Byers took up again quite smoothly. "You know, Franz, I've always been impressed by how in London's last great novel *The Star Rover* mind triumphs completely over matter. By frightfully intense self-discipline a lifer at San Quentin is enabled to escape in spirit through the thick walls of his prison and move at will through the world and relive his past reincarnations, re-die his deaths. Somehow that makes me think of old de Castries in the 1920s, living alone in downtown cheap hotels and brooding, brooding, brooding about past hopes and glories and disasters. And (dreaming the while of foul unending tortures) about the wrongs done to him and about revenge (whether or not he actually worked something there) and about . . . who knows what else? sending his mind upon . . . who knows what journeys?

"During this period we must picture him as a bent old man, so taciturn most of the time, always depressed, and getting paranoid. For instance, now he had a thing about never touching metal surfaces and fixtures, because his enemies were trying to electrocute him. Sometimes he was afraid they were poisoning his tap water in the pipes. He seldom would go out, for fear a car would jump the curb and get him, and he no longer spry enough to dodge, or an enemy would shatter his skull with a brick or tile dropped from a high roof. At the same time he was frequently changing his hotel, to throw them off his trail. Now his only contacts with former associates were his dogged attempts to get back and burn all copies of his book, though there may still have been some blackmailing and plain begging. Ricker and Klaas witnessed one such book burning. Grotesque affair!—he burned two copies in his bathtub. They remembered opening the windows and fanning out the smoke. With one or two exceptions, they were his only visitors—lonely and eccentric types themselves and already failed men like himself although they were only in their thirties at the time.

"Then Clark Ashton Smith came, the same age, but brimming with poetry and imagination and creative energy.

He'd been hard hit by George Sterling's nasty death and had felt driven to look up such friends and acquaintances of his poetic mentor as he could find. De Castries felt old fires stir. Here was another of the brilliant, vitalic ones he'd always sought. He was tempted (finally yielding entirely) to exert his formidable charm for a last time, to tell his fabulous tales, to expand compellingly his eerie theories, and to weave his spells.

"And Clark Ashton Smith, a lover of the weird and of its beauty, highly intelligent, yet in some ways still a naïve small-town youth, emotionally turbulent, made a most gratifying audience. For several weeks Clark delayed his return to Auburn, fearfully reveling in the ominous, wonder-shot, strangely *real* world that old Tiberius, the scarecrow emperor of terror and mysteries, painted for him afresh each day—a San Francisco of spectral though rock-solid mega buildings and invisible paramental entities more real than life. It's easy to see why the Tiberius metaphor caught Clark's fancy. At one point he wrote—Hold on for a moment, Franz, while I get that photocopy—"

"There's no need," Franz said, dragging the journal itself out of his side pocket. The binoculars came out with it and dropped to the thickly carpeted floor with a shivery little clash of the broken glass inside.

Byers' eyes followed them with morbid curiosity. "So those are the glasses that (take warning, Franz!) several times saw a paramental entity and were in the end destroyed by it." His gaze shifted to the journal. "Franz, you sly dog! You came prepared for at least part of this discussion before you ever went to Corona Heights today!"

Franz picked up the binoculars and put them on the low table beside his overflowing ashtray, meanwhile glancing rapidly around the room and at its windows, where the gold had darkened a little. He said quietly, "It seems to me, Donaldus, you've been holding out too. You take for granted now that Smith wrote the journal. but in the Haight and even in the letters we exchanged afterwards, you said you were uncertain."

"You've got me," Byers admitted with a rather odd little smile, perhaps ashamed. "But it really seemed *wise*, Franz, to let as few people in on it as possible. Now of course you know as much as I do, or will in a few minutes, but . . . The most camp of clichés is 'There are some things man was not meant to know', but there are times when I believe it really applies to Thibaut de Castries and the paranatural. Might I see the journal?"

Franz flipped it across. Byers caught it as if it were made of eggshell, and with an aggrieved look at his guest carefully opened it and as carefully turned a couple of pages. "Yes, here it is. 'Three hours today at 607 Rhodes. What a locus for genius! How prosaick!—as Howard would spell it. And yet Tiberius is Tiberius indeed, miserly doling out his dark Thrasyllus secrets in this canyoned, cavernous Capri called San Francisco to his frightened young heir (God, no! Not I!) Caligula. And wondering how soon I too will go mad.' "

As he finished reading aloud, Byers began to turn the next pages, one at a time, and kept it up even when he came to the blank ones. Now and then he'd look up at Franz, but he examined each page minutely with fingers and eyes before he turned it.

He said conversationally, "Clark did think of San Francisco as a modern Rome, you know, both cities with their seven hills. From Auburn he'd seen George Sterling and the rest living as if all life were a Roman holiday. With Carmel perhaps analogous to Capri, which was simply Tiberius's Little Rome, for the more advanced fun and games. Fishermen brought fresh caught lobsters to the goatish old emperor; Sterling dove for giant abalone with his knife.

Of course, Rhodes was the Capri of Tiberius' early middle years. No, I can see why Clark would not have wanted to be Caligula. 'Art, like the bartender, is never drunk'—or really schiz. Hello, what's this?"

His fingernails were gently teasing at the edge of a page. "It's clear you're not a bibliophile, dear Franz. I should have gone ahead and stolen the book from you that evening in the Haight, as at one point I fully intended to, except that something gallant in your drunken manner touched my conscience, which is never a good guide to follow. There!"

With the ghostliest of cracklings the page came apart into two, revealing writing hidden between.

He reported, "It's black as new—India ink for certain—but done very lightly so as not to groove the paper in the slightest. Then a few tiny drops of gum arabic, not enough to wrinkle, and—hey presto!—it's hidden quite neatly. The obscurity of the obvious. 'Upon their vestments is a writing no man may see . . . ' *Oh, dear me, no!*"

He resolutely averted his eyes, which had been reading while he spoke. Then he stood up and holding the journal at arm's length came over and squatted on his hams, so close beside Franz that his brandy breath was obvious, and held the newly liberated page spread before their faces. Only the right-hand one was written upon, its very black yet spider-fine characters very neatly drawn and not remotely like Smith's handwriting.

"Thank you," Franz said. "This is weird. I riffled through those pages a dozen times."

"But you did not examine each one minutely with the true bibliophile's profound mistrust. The signatory initials indicate it was written by old Tiberius himself. And I'm sharing this with you not so much out of courtesy, as fear. Glancing at the opening, I got the feeling this was something I did not want to read all by myself."

Together they silently read the following:

A CURSE upon Master Clark Ashton Smith and all his heirs, who thought to pick my brain and slip away, false fleeting agent of my old enemies. Upon him the Long Death, the paramental agony! when he strays back as all men do. The fulcrum (0) and the Cipher (A) shall be here, at his *beloved* 607 Rhodes. I'll be at rest in my appointed spot (1) under the Bishop's Seat, the heaviest ashes that he ever felt. Then when the weights are on at Sutro Mount (4) and Monkey Clay (5) [(4) + (1) = (5)] *BE his Life Squeezed Away.* Committed to Cipher in my 50-Book (A). Go out, my little book (B), into the world, and lie in wait in stalls and lurk on shelves for the unwary purchaser. Go out, my little book, and break some necks!

As he finished reading it, Franz's mind was whirling with so many names of places and things both familiar and strange that he had to prod himself to remind himself to check visually the windows and doors and corners of Byers' gorgeous living room, now filling with shadows. That business about "when the weights are on", he couldn't imagine what it meant, but taken together with "heaviest ashes" it made him think of the old man pressed to death with heavy stones on a plank on his chest for refusing to testify at the Salem witchcraft trial of 1692, as if a confession could be forced out like a last breath.

"Monkey Clay," Byers muttered puzzledly. "Ape of clay? Poor suffering Man, molded of dust?"

Franz shook his head. And in the midst of all, he thought, that damnably puzzling 607 Rhodes! Which kept turning up again and again, and had in a way touched all this off.

And to think he'd had this book for years and not spotted the secret. It made a person suspect and distrust all things closest to him, his most familiar possessions. What might not be hidden inside the lining of your clothes, or in your right-hand trousers' pocket (or for a woman, in her handbag or bra), or in the cake of soap with which you washed (which might have a razor blade inside).

Also to think that he was looking at last at de Castries' own handwriting, so neatly drawn and yet so crabbed for all that.

One detail puzzled him differently. "Donaldus," he said, "how would de Castries ever have got hold of Smith's journal?"

Byers let out a long, alcohol-laden sigh, massaged his face with his hands (Franz clutched the journal to keep it from falling) and said, "Oh, that. Klaas and Ricker both told me that de Castries was quite worried and hurt when Clark went back to Auburn (it turned out) without warning after visiting the old man every day for a month or so. De Castries was so bothered, they said, that he went over to Clark's cheap rooming house and convinced them he was Clark's uncle, so that they gave him some things Clark had left behind when he'd checked out in a great tearing hurry the day before. 'I'll keep them for little Clark,' he told Klaas and Ricker, and then later (after they'd heard from Clark) he added, 'I've shipped him back his things.' They never suspected that the old man ever entertained any hard feelings about Clark."

Franz nodded. "But then how did the journal (now with the curse in it) get from de Castries to wherever I bought it?"

Byers said wearily, "Who knows? The curse, though, does remind me of another side of de Castries' character I haven't mentioned: his fondness for rather cruel practical jokes. Despite his morbid fear of electricity, he had a chair Ricker helped rig for him to give the sitter an electric shock through the cushion that he kept for salesmen and salesladies, children, and other stray visitors. He nearly got into police trouble through that too. Some young lady looking for typing work got her bottom burned," Byers finished and stood up, leaving the journal in Franz's hands, and went back to his place. Franz looked at him questioningly, holding out the journal toward him a little, but his host said, pouring himself more brandy, "No, you keep it. It's yours. After all, you were—are—the purchaser. Only, for Heaven's sake, take better care of it! It's a *very* rare item."

"But what do you think of it, Donaldus?" Franz asked.

The other shrugged as he began to sip. "A shivery document indeed," he said, smiling at Franz as if he were very glad the latter had it. "And it really did lie in wait in stalls and lurk on shelves for many years, apparently. Franz, don't you recall *anything* about where you bought it?"

"I've tried and tried," Franz said tormentedly. "The place was in the Haight, I'm fairly sure of that. Called . . . the In Group? The Black Spot? The Black Dog? The Grey Cockatoo? No, none of those, and I've tried hundreds of names. I think that 'black' was in it, but I believe the proprietor was a white man. And there was a little girl, maybe his daughter, helping him. Not so little, really—she was into puberty, I seem to recall, and well aware of it. Pushing herself at me—all this is very vague. I also seem to recall (I was drunk of course) being attracted to her," he confessed somewhat ashamedly.

"My dear Franz, aren't we all?" Byers observed. "The little darlings, barely kissed by sex, but don't they know it! Who can resist? Do you recall what you paid for the books?"

"Something pretty high, I think. But now I'm beginning to guess and imagine."

"You could search through the Haight, street by street, of course."

"I suppose I could, if it's still there and hasn't changed its name. Why don't you get on with your story, Donaldus?"

"Very well. There's not much more of it. You know, Franz, there's one indication that that . . . er . . . curse isn't particularly efficacious. Clark lived a long and productive life, thirty-three more years. Reassuring, don't you think?"

"He didn't stray back to San Francisco," Franz said shortly. "At least not very often."

"That's true. Well, after Clark left, de Castries remained . . . just a lonely and gloomy old man. He once told George Ricker at about this time a very unromantic story of his past: that he was French Canadian and had grown up in northern Vermont, his father by turns a small-town printer and a farmer, always a failure, and he a lonely and unhappy child. It has the ring of truth, don't you think? Well, anyhow, now he'd had his last fling (with Clark) at playing the omnipotent sinister sorcerer, and it had turned out as bitterly as it had the first time in fin de siècle San Francisco (if that was the first). Gloomy and lonely. He only had one other literary acquaintance at that time, or friend of any sort, for that matter. Klaas and Ricker both vouch for it. Dashiell Hammett, who was living in San Francisco in an apartment at Post and Hyde, and writing *The Maltese Falcon*. Those bookstore names you were trying out reminded me of it—the Black Dog and a cockatoo. You see, the fabulously jewelled gold falcon painted black (and finally proven a fake) is sometimes called the Black Bird in Hammett's detective story. He and de Castries talked a lot about black treasures, Klaas and Ricker told me. And about the historical background of Hammett's book—the Knights Hospitalers (later of Malta) who created the falcon and how they'd once been the Knights of Rhodes—"

"Rhodes turning up again!" Franz interjected. "That damn 607 Rhodes!"

"Yes," Byers agreed. "First Tiberius, then the Hospitalers. They held the island for two hundred years and were finally driven out of it by the sultan Mohammed II in 1522. But about the Black Bird—you'll recall what I told you of de Castries' *pietra dura* ring of mosaicked black semiprecious stuff depicting a black bird? Klaas claims it was the inspiration for *The Maltese Falcon*! One needn't go that far, of course, but just the same it's all very odd indeed, don't you think? De Castries and Hammett. The black magician and the tough detective."

"Not so odd as all that when you think about it," Franz countered, his eyes on one of their roving trips again. "Besides being one of America's few great novelists, Hammett was a rather lonely and taciturn man himself, with an almost fabulous integrity. He elected to serve a sentence in a federal prison rather than betray a trust. And he enlisted in World War II when he didn't have to and served it out in the cold Aleutians and finally toughed out a long last illness. No, he'd have been interested in a queer old duck like de Castries and showed a hard, unsentimental compassion toward his loneliness and bitterness and failures. Go on, Donaldus."

"There's really nothing more," the latter said, but his eyes were flashing. "De Castries died of a coronary occlusion in 1929 after two weeks in the City Hospital. It happened in the summertime—I remember Klaas saying the old man didn't even live to see the stock market crash and the beginnings of the Great Depression, 'which would have been a comfort to him because it would have confirmed his theories that because of the self-abuse of mega-cities, the world was going to hell in a hand basket.'

"So that was that. De Castries was cremated, as he'd wished, which took his last cash. Ricker and Klaas split his few possessions. There were of course no relatives."

"I'm glad of that," Franz said. "I mean, that he was cremated. Oh, I know he died—had to be dead after all these years—but just the same, along with all the rest today, I've had this picture of de Castries, a very old man, but wiry and somehow very fast, still slipping around San Francisco. Hearing that he not only died in a hospital but was cremated makes his death more final."

"In a way," Byers agreed, giving him an odd look. "Klaas had the ashes sitting just inside his front door for a while in a cheap canister the crematory had furnished, until he and Ricker figured out what to do with them. They finally decided to follow de Castries' wish there too, although it meant an illegal burial and doing it all secretly at night. Ricker carried a post-digger packaged in newspaper, and Klaas a small spade, similarly wrapped.

"There were two other persons in the funeral party. Dashiell Hammett—he decided a question for them, as it happened. They'd been arguing as to whether de Castries' black ring (Klaas had it) should be buried with the ashes, and so they put it up to Hammett, and he said, 'Of course.' "

"That figures," Franz said, nodding. "But how very strange."

"Yes, wasn't it?" Byers agreed. "The fourth person—he even carried the ashes—was Clark. I thought that would surprise you. They'd got in touch with him in Auburn and he'd come back just for that night. It shows, come to think of it, that Clark couldn't have known about the curse—or does it? Anyhow, the little burial detail set forth from Klaas's place just after dark. It was a clear night and the moon was gibbous, a few days before full—which was a good thing, as they had some climbing to do where there were no street lights."

Byers looked at Franz with a sort of relish and finished rapidly. "The burial went off without a hitch, though they needed the post-digger—the ground was hard. The only thing lacking was the TV tower, that fantastic cross between a dressmaker's dummy and a Burmese pagoda in the feast of red lanterns, to lean down through the night and give a cryptic blessing. The spot was just below a natural rock seat that de Castries had called the Bishop's Seat after the one in Poe's *Gold-Bug* story, and just at the base of the big rock outcropping that is the summit of Corona Heights. Oh, incidentally—another of his whims they gratified—he was burned wearing a bathrobe he'd worn to tatters—a pale old brown one with a cowl."

Franz's eyes, engaged in one of their roving all-inspections, got the command to check the glooms and shadows not only for a pale, blank, triangular face with restless snout, but also for the thin, hawkish, ghostly one, tormented and tormenting, murder-bent, of a hyperactive old man looking like something out of Doré's illustrations to Dante's *Inferno*. Since he'd never seen a photograph of de Castries, if any existed, that would have to do.

His mind was busy assimilating the thought that Corona Heights was literally impregnated with Thibaut de Castries. That both yesterday and today he had occupied for rather long periods of time what must almost certainly be the Bishop's Seat of the curse, while only a few yards below in the hard ground were the essential dusts (salts?) and the black ring. How did that go in the cipher in Poe's tale? "Take a good glass in the Bishop's Seat . . . " His glasses were broken, but then he hardly needed them for this short-range work. Which were worse, ghosts or paramentals?—or were they, conceivably, the same? When one was simply on watch for the approach of both or either, that was a rather academic question, no matter how many interesting problems it posed about different levels of reality. Somewhere, deep down, he was aware of being angry, or perhaps only argumentative.

"Turn on some lights, Donaldus," he said in a flat voice.

"I must say, you're taking it very coolly," the other said in slightly aggrieved, slightly awed tones.

"What do you expect me to do, panic? Run out in the street and get shot?—or crushed by falling walls? or cut by flying glass? I suppose, Donaldus, that you delayed revealing the exact location of de Castries' grave so that it would have a greater dramatic impact, and so be truer, in line with your theory of the identity of reality and art?"

"Exactly! You *do* understand, and I *did* tell you there would be a ghost and how appropriately the astrological graffiti served as Thibaut's epitaph, or tomb décor. But isn't it all so very *amazing*, Franz? To think that when you first looked from your window at Corona Heights, Thibaut de Castries' mortal remains unknown to you—"

"Turn on some lights," Franz repeated. "What I find amazing, Donaldus, is that you've known about paramental entities for many years, and about the highly sinister activities of de Castries and the suggestive circumstances of his burial, and yet take no more precautions against them than you do. You're like a soldier dancing the light fantastic in No Man's Land. Always remembering that I, or you, or both of us may at this moment be totally insane. Of course, you only learned about the curse just now, if I can trust you. And you did bolt the door after I came in. Turn on some lights!"

Byers complied at last. A dull gold refulgence streamed from the large globular shade suspended above them. He moved to the front hall, somewhat reluctantly, it appeared, and flicked a switch, then to the back of the living room, where he did the same and then busied himself opening another bottle of brandy. The windows became dark rectangles netted with gold. Full night had fallen. But at least the shadows inside had been banished.

All this while he was saying in a voice that had grown rather listless and dispirited now that his tale had been told, "Of course you can trust me, Franz. It was out of consideration for your own safety that I didn't tell you about de Castries. Until today, when it became clear you were into the business, like it or not. I don't go babbling about it all, believe me. If I've learned one thing over the years, it's that it's a mercy *not* to tell anyone about the darker side of de Castries and his theories. That's why I've never even *considered* publishing a monograph about the man. What other reason could I have for that?—such a book would be brilliant. Fa Lo Suee knows all—one can't hide anything from a serious lover—but she has a very strong mind, as I've suggested. In fact, after you called this morning, I suggested to her as she was going out that if she had some spare time she have another look for the bookstore where you bought the journal—she has a talent for such problems. She smiled and said that, as it happened, she'd been planning to do just that."

"Donaldus," Franz said sharply, "you've been a lot deeper and more steadily into this all along than you've told me— and your girlfriend too, apparently."

"Companion," Byers corrected. "Or, if you will, lover. Yes, that's right—it's been one of my chief secondary concerns (primary now) for quite a few years. But what was I saying? Oh, yes, that Fa Lo Suee knows all. So did a couple of her predecessors—a famous interior decorator and a tennis star who was also an actor. Clark, Klaas, and Ricker knew—they were my source—but they're all dead. So you see I do try to shield others—and myself up to a point. I regard paramental entities as very real and present dangers, about midway in nature between the atomic bomb and the archetypes of the collective unconscious, which include several highly dangerous characters, as you know. Or between a Charles Manson or a Zodiac killer and kappa phenomena as defined by Meleta Denning in *Gnostica*. Or between muggers and elementals, or hepatitis viruses and incubi. They're all of them things any sane man is on guard against.

"But mark this, Franz," he emphasized, pouring out brandy, "despite all my previous knowledge, so much more extensive and of such longer standing than your own, I've never actually *seen* a paramental entity. You have the advantage of me there. And it seems to be *quite* an advantage." And he looked at Franz with a mixture of avidity and dread.

Franz stood up. "Perhaps it is," he said shortly, "at least in making a person stay on guard. You say you're trying to protect yourself, but you don't act that way. Right now— excuse me, Donaldus—you're getting so drunk that you'd be helpless if a paramental entity—"

The other's eyebrows went up. "You think you could defend yourself against them, resist them, fight them, destroy them?" he asked incredulously, his voice strengthening. "Can you stop an atomic missile headed for San Francisco at this moment through the ionosphere? Can you command the germs of cholera? Can you abolish your Anima or your Shadow? Can you say to the poltergeist 'Don't knock?' You can't stand guard twenty-four hours a day for months, for years. Believe me, I know. A soldier crouched in a dugout can't try to figure out if the next shell will be a direct hit or not. He'd go crazy if he tried. No, Franz, all you can do is lock the doors and windows, turn on all the lights, and hope they pass you by. And try to forget them. Eat, drink, and be merry. Recreate yourself. Here, have a drink."

He came toward Franz carrying in each hand a glass half full of brandy.

"No, thank you," Franz said harshly, jamming the journal into his coat pocket, to Byers' fleeting distress. Then he picked up the tinkling binoculars and jammed them in the other side pocket, thinking in a flash of the binoculars in James's ghost story "A View from a Hill" that had been magicked to see the past by being filled with a black fluid from boiled bones that had oozed out nastily when they were broken. Could his own binoculars have been somehow doctored or gimmicked so that they saw things that weren't there? A wildly far-fetched notion, and anyhow his own binoculars were broken too.

"I'm sorry, Donaldus, but I've got to go," he said, heading for the hall. He knew that if he stayed he *would* take a drink, starting the old cycle, and the idea of becoming unconscious *and incapable of being roused* was very repellent.

Byers hurried after him. His haste and his gyrations to keep the brandy from spilling would have been comic under other circumstances and if he hadn't been saying in a horrified, plaintive, pleading voice: "You can't go out, it's dark. You can't go out with that old devil or his paramental slipping around. Here, have a drink and stay the night. At least stay for the party. If you're going to stand on guard, you're going to need some rest and recreation. I'm sure you'll find an agreeable and pleasing partner—they'll all be swingers, but intelligent. And if you're afraid of liquor dulling your mind, I've some cocaine, the purest crystal." He drained one glass and set it down on the hall table. "Look, Franz, I'm frightened too—and you've been pale ever since I told you where the old devil's dust is laid. Stay for the party. And have just one drink—enough to relax a little. In the end there's no other way, believe me. You'd just get too tired, trying to watch forever." He swayed a little, wheedling, smiling his pleasantest.

A weight of weariness descended on Franz. He reached toward the glass, but just as he touched it he jerked his fingers away as if they'd been burned.

"Shh," he cautioned as Byers started to speak and he warningly gripped him by the elbow. In the silence they heard a tiny, faintly grating, sliding metallic sound ending in a soft snap, as of a key being rotated in a lock. Their eyes went to the front door. They saw the brass inner knob revolve.

"It's Fa Lo Suee," Byers said. "I'll have to unbolt the door." He moved to do so.

"Wait!" Franz whispered urgently. "Listen!"

They heard a steady scratching sound that didn't end, as if some intelligent beast were drawing a horny claw round and round on the other side of the painted wood. There rose unbidden in Franz's imagination the paralyzing image of a large black panther crouched close against the other side of the gold-traced white opacity, a green-eyed, gleamingly black panther that was beginning to metamorphose into something more terrible.

"Up to her tricks," Byers muttered and drew the bolt before Franz could move to hinder him.

The door pressed halfway open, and around it came two pale-gray, triangular flat feline faces that glittered at the edges and were screeching "Aiii-eee!" it sounded.

Both men recoiled, Franz flinching aside with eyes involuntarily slitted from two pale-gray gleaming shapes, a taller and a slenderer one, that whirled past him as they shot menacingly at Byers, who was bent half double in his retreat, one arm thrown shielding across his eyes, the other across his groin, while the gleaming wine glass and the small sheet of amber fluid it had contained still sailed through the air from the point where his hand had abandoned them.

Incongruously, Franz's mind registered the odors of brandy, burnt hemp, and a spicy perfume. The gray shapes converged on Byers, clutching at his groin, and as he gasped and gabbled inarticulately, weakly trying to fend them off, the taller was saying in a husky contralto voice with great enjoyment, "In China, Mr. Nayland Smith, we have ways to make men talk."

Then the brandy was on the pale green wallpaper, the unbroken wine glass on the golden-brown carpet, and the stoned, handsome Chinese woman and equally mind-blown urchin-faced girl had snatched off their gray cat-masks, though laughing wildly and continuing to grope and tickle Byers vigorously; and Franz realized they had both been screeching "Jaime," his host's first name, at the top of their voices.

His extreme fear had left Franz, but not its paralysis. The latter extended to his vocal cords, so that from the moment of the strange eruption of the two gray-clad females to the moment when he left the house on Beaver Street he never spoke a word but only stood beside the dark rectangle of the open door and observed the busy tableau farther down the hall with a rather cold detachment.

Fa Lo Suee had a spare, somewhat angular figure, a flat face with strong bony structure, dark eyes that were para-doxically both bright and dull with marijuana (and what-ever) and straight, dull black hair. Her dark red lips were thin. She wore silver-gray stockings and gloves and a closely fitting dress (of ribbed silver-gray silk) of the Chinese sort that always looks modern. Her left hand threatened Byers in his midst, her right lay loosely low around the slender waist of her companion.

The latter was a head shorter, almost but not quite skin-ny, and had sexy little breasts. Her face was actually catlike: receding chin, pouty lips, a snub nose, protuberant blue eyes and low forehead, from which straight blonde hair fell to one side. She looked about seventeen, bratty and worldly-wise. She plinked a note in Franz's memory. She wore a pale-gray leotard, silver-gray gloves, and a gray cloak of some light material that now hung to one side like her hair. Both of her hands mischievously groped Byers. She had a pink ear and a vicious giggle.

The two gray cat-masks, cast on the hall table now, were edged with silver sequins and had a few stiff whiskers, but they retained the nasty triangular snouty appearance which had been so unnerving coming around the door.

Donaldus (or Jaime) spoke no really intelligible word himself during this period before Franz's departure, except perhaps "Don't!" but he gasped and squealed and babbled a lot, with breathless little laughs thrown in. He stayed bent half double and twisting from side to side, his hands constantly but rather ineffectually fending off the clutching ones. His pale violet dressing gown, unbelted, swished as he twisted.

It was the women who did all the talking and at first only Fa Lo Suee. "We really scared you, didn't we?" she said rapidly. "Jaime scares easily, Shirl, especially when he's drunk. That was my key scratching the door. Go on, Shirl, give it to him!" Then resuming her Fu Manchu voice, "What have you and Dr. Petrie there been up to? In Honan, Mr. Nayland Smith, we have an infallible Chinese test for homophilia. Or is it possible you're AC-DC? We have the ancient wisdom of the East, all the dark lore that Mao Tse-tung's forgotten. Combined with western science, it's devastating. (That's it, girl, hurt him!) Remember my thugs and dacoits, Mr. Smith, my golden scorpions and red six-inch centipedes, my black spiders with diamond eyes that wait in the dark, then leap! How would you like one of those dropped down your pants? Repeat, what have you and Dr. Petrie been doing? Be careful what you say. My assistant, Miss Shirley Soames (keep it up, Shirl!), has a rat-trap memory. No lie will go unnoticed."

Franz, frozen, felt rather as if he were watching crayfish and sea anemones scuttling and grasping, fronds questing, pincers and flower-mouths opening and closing, in a rock pool. The endless play of life.

"Oh, by the bye, Jaime, I've solved the problem of the Smith journal," Fa Lo Suee said in a bright casual voice while her own hands became more active. "This is Shirl Soames, Jaime (you're getting to him, girl!), who for years and years has been her father's assistant at the Gray's Inn bookstore in the Haight. And she remembers the whole transaction, although it was four years ago, because she has a *rat-trap* memory."

The name "Gray's Inn" lit up like neon in Franz's mind. How had he kept missing it?

"Oh, traps distress you, do they, Nayland Smith?" Fa Lo Suee went on. "They're cruel to animals, are they? Western sentimentality! I will have you know, for your information, that Shirl Soames here can *bite*, as well as nip exquisitely."

As she was saying that, she was sliding her silk-gloved right hand down the girl's rump and inward, until the tip of her middle finger appeared to be resting on the spot midway between the outer orifices of the reproductive and digestive systems. The girl appreciatively jogged her hips from side to side through a very short arc.

Franz took coldly clinical note of those actions and of the inward fact that under other circumstances it would have been an exciting gesture, making him want to do so himself to Shirley Soames, and so be done by. But why her in particular? Memories stirred.

Fa Lo Suee noticed Franz and turned her head. Giving him a very civilized, glassy-eyed smile, she said politely, "Ah, you must be Franz Westen, the writer, who phoned Jaime this morning. So you as well as he will be interested in what Shirley has to say. "Shirl, leave off excruciating Jaime. He's had enough punishment. Is this the gentleman?" And without removing her hand she gently swung the girl around until she faced Franz.

Behind them Byers, still bent over, was taking deep breaths mixed with dying chuckles as he began to recover from the working over he'd been given.

With amphetamine-bright eyes the girl looked Franz up and down. While he was realizing that he knew that feline, foxy little face (face of a cat, presently licking cream), though on a body skinnier still and another head shorter.

"That's him, all right," she said in a rapid, sharp voice that still had something of a brat's "yah! yah!" in it. "Correct, mister? Four years ago you bought two old books tied together out of a lot that had been around for years that my father'd bought that'd belonged to a George Ricker. You were squiffed, really skew-iffed! You paid $25. I thought you thought you were paying for a chance to feel me up. Were you? So many of the older men wanted to. I was Daddy's star attraction, and didn't he know it! But I'd already found out girls were nicer."

All this while she'd continued to jog her little hips lasciviously, leaning back a little, and now she slipped her own right hand behind her, presumably to rest it on Fa Lo Suee's.

Franz looked at Shirley Soames and at the two others, and he knew that all that she had said was true, and he also knew that this was how Jaime Donaldus Byers escaped from his fears (and Fa Lo Suee from hers?). And without a word or any change in his rather stupid expression he turned and walked out the open door.

He had a sharp pang—"I am abandoning Donaldus!"— and a fleeting thought—"Would Fa Lo Suee immortalize the exquisite moment in slim silver, perhaps titling it 'The Loving Goose'?"—but neither made him pause or reconsider. As he started down the steps, light from the doorway spilling around him, his eyes were already systematically checking the darkness ahead for hostile presences—each corner, each yawning areaway, each shadowy rooftop, each coign of vantage. As he reached the street, the soft light around him vanished as the door behind him was silently shut. That relieved him—it made him less of a target in the full onyx dusk that had now closed once more on San Francisco.

As he moved cautiously down Beaver Street, his eyes checking the glooms between the rather few lights, his mind thought of how de Castries had ceased to be a mere parochial devil haunting the lonely hump of Corona Heights (and Franz's own room at 811 Geary?), but a ubiquitous demon, ghost, or paramental inhabiting the whole city with its scattered humping hills. For that matter, to keep it all materialistic, were not some of the atoms shed from de Castries' body during his life and during his burial forty years ago around Franz here at this very moment and in the very air that he was discretely sniffing in?—atoms being so vastly tiny and infinity-numerous. As were the atoms too of Francis Drake (sailing past San Francisco Bay-to-be in the *Golden Hind*) and of Shakespeare and Socrates and Solomon (and of Dashiell Hammett and Clark Ashton Smith). And for that matter, too, had not the atoms that were to become Thibaut de Castries been circulating around the world before the pyramids were built?—slowly converging on the spot (in Vermont? in France?) where the old devil would be born? And before that, had not those Thibaut atoms been swiftly vectoring from the violent birthplace of the universe to the space-time spot where earth would be born and all its weird Pandora woes?

Blocks off, a siren yelped. Nearby, a dark cat darted into a black slit between walls set too close for human passage. It made Franz think of how big buildings had been threatening to crush man ever since the first mega-city had been built. Really Saul's crazy (?) Mrs. Willis wasn't so far off the track, nor Lovecraft (and Smith?) with his fascinated dread of vast rooms with ceilings that were indoor skies and far walls that were horizons, in buildings vaster still. San Francisco was carbuncled with the latter, and each month new ones grew. Were the signs of the universe written into them? Whose wandering atoms didn't they hold? And were paramentals their personification or their vermin or their natural predators? In any case, it all transpired as logically and ineluctably as the rice-paper journal had passed from Smith, who wrote in purple ink, to de Castries, who added a deadly, secret black, to Ricker, who was a locksmith not a bibliophile, to Soames, who had a precociously sexy daughter, to Westen, who was susceptible to weird and sexy things.

A dark-blue taxi coasting slowly and silently downhill ghosted by Franz and drew up at the opposite curb. No wonder Donaldus had wanted Franz to keep the journal and its new-found curse! Byers was an old campaigner against paramentals, with his defense in depth of locks and lights, and liquor, drugs, and sex, and outré sex—Fa Lo Suee had brought Shirley Soames for him as well as for herself; the humorously hostile groping had been to cheer him. Very resourceful, truly. A person had to sleep. Maybe he'd learn, Franz told himself, to use the Byers method himself someday, minus the liquor, but not tonight, no, not until he had to.

The headlights of an unseen car on Noe illuminated the corner ahead at the foot of Beaver. While Franz scanned for shapes that might have been hiding in the dark and now revealed, he thought of Donaldus' inner defense perimeter, meaning his aesthetic approach to life, his theory that art and reality, fiction and nonfiction, were all one, so that one needn't waste energy distinguishing them.

But wasn't even that defense a rationalization, Franz asked himself, an attempt to escape facing the overwhelming question that you're led to: *Are paramentals real?*

Yet how could you answer that question when you were on the run and getting weary and wearier? And then Franz suddenly saw how he could escape for now, at least buy time in which to think in safety. And it did not involve liquor, drugs, or sex, or diminishing watchfulness in any way. He touched his pocketbook and felt inside it—yes, there was the ticket. He struck a match and glanced at his watch—not yet quite eight, still time enough if he moved swiftly. He turned. The dark-blue cab, having discharged its passenger, was coming down Beaver with its hire light on. He stepped into the street and waved it down. He started to get in, then hesitated. A searching glance told him that the dusky, lustrous interior was empty. He got inside and slammed the door, noting approvingly that the windows were closed.

"The Civic Center," he directed. "The Veterans Building. There is a concert there."

"Oh, one of those," the driver said, an older man. "If you don't mind, I won't take Market, it's too torn up. Going around, we'll get there quicker."

"That's fine," Franz said, settling back as the cab turned north on Noe and speeded up. He knew, or had been assuming, that ordinary physical laws didn't apply to paramentals, even if they were real, and so that being in a swiftly moving vehicle didn't make his situation any safer, but it felt that way—it helped.

The familiar drama of a cab ride took hold of him a little—the dark house fronts and store fronts shooting past, the slowings at the bright corners, the red-green race with the stop lights. But he still kept scanning, regularly swinging his head to look behind, now to the left, now to the right.

"When I was a kid here," the driver said, "they didn't use to tear up Market so much. But now they do it all the time. That BART. And other streets too. All those damn high rises. We'd be better off without them."

"I'm with you there," Franz said.

"You and me both," the driver confirmed. "The driving'd sure be easier. Watch it, you bastard."

The last rather mildly spoken remark was intended for a car that was trying to edge into the right lane on McAllister, though hardly for the ears of its driver. Down a side street Franz saw a huge orange globe glowing aloft like a Jupiter that was all one Red Spot—advertisement of a Union 76 gas station. They turned on Van Ness and immediately drew up at the curb. Franz paid his fare, adding a generous tip, and crossed the wide sidewalk to the Veterans Building and through its wide glass door into its lofty lobby set with eight-inch diameter tubular modernistic sculptures like giant metal worms at war.

With a few other late-coming concertgoers he hurried to the elevator at the back, feeling both claustrophobia and relief as the slow doors closed. On the fourth floor they joined the other last-minute folk giving up their tickets and taking their programs before entering the medium-size high, bone-white hall with its rows of chairs, now mostly occupied.

At first the press of people bothered Franz (anyone might be, or hide, anything) but rather swiftly began to reassure him by their concert-normality: the mostly conservative clothes, whether Establishment or Hippy; the scatter of elven folk in arty garb suitable for rarefied artistic experiences; the elderly groups, the ladies in sober evening dresses with a touch of silver, the gentlemen rather fussily clad at collars and cuffs.

A very aware and coldly calculating section of Franz's mind told him that he was not one bit safer here than out in the dark. Nevertheless his fears were being lulled as they had been when he'd first arrived at Beaver Street and later, a little, in the cab.

He heard his name called, started, then hurried down an aisle to where Gunnar and Saul were holding a seat between them in the third row.

"It's about time," Saul said darkly as Franz edged past.

As he sat down, Gun said from the seat just beyond, grinning somewhat thinly and momentarily laying his hand on Franz's forearms, "We were beginning to get afraid you weren't coming. You know how much Cal depends on you, don't you?" Then a puzzled question came into his face when the glass in Franz's pocket clashed as he pulled his jacket round.

"I broke my binoculars on Corona Heights," Franz said shortly. "I'll tell you about it later." Then a thought came to him. "Do you know much about optics, Gun? Practical optics—instruments and such, prisms and lenses?"

"A little," Gun replied, with an inquiring frown. "And I've a friend who's very much into it."

Franz said slowly, "Would it be possible to gimmick a terrestrial telescope, or a pair of binoculars, so a person would see something in the distance that wasn't there?"

"Well . . . " Gunnar began, his expression wondering, his hands making a small gesture of uncertainty. Then he smiled. "Of course, if you tried to look through broken binoculars, I suppose you'd see something like a kaleidoscope."

"Taffy get rough?" Saul asked from the other side.

"Never mind now," Franz told Gunnar and with a quick, temporizing grimace at Saul (and a quick glance behind him and to either side—crowded concertgoers and their coats made such an effective stalking ground) and he looked toward the stage, where the half dozen or so instrumentalists were already seated—in a shallow, concave curve just beyond the conductor's podium, one of the strings still tuning thoughtfully. The long and narrow shape of the harpsichord, its slim bench empty, made the left end of the curve, somewhat downstage to favor its small tones.

Franz looked at his program. The Brandenburg Fifth was the finale. There were two intermissions. The concert opened with:

Concerto in C Major for Harpsichord and
Chamber Orchestra by Giovanni Paisiello
    1. Allegro
    2. Larghetto
    3. Allegro (Rondo)

Saul nudged him. He looked up. Cal had come on stage unobtrusively. She wore a white evening frock that left her shoulders bare and sparkled just a little at the edges. She said something to a woodwind and in turning looked the audience over without making a point of it. He thought she saw him, but he couldn't be sure. She seated herself. The house lights went down. To a spreading ripple of applause the conductor entered, took his place, looked around from under his eyebrows at his instrumentalists, tapped the lectern with his wand, and raised it sharply.

Beside Franz, Saul murmured prayerfully, "Now in the name of Bach and Sigmund Freud, give 'em hell, Calpurnia!"

"And of Pythagoras," Gun faintly chimed.

The sweet and rocking music of the strings and of the softly calling, lulling woodwinds enfolded Franz. For the first time since Corona Heights he felt wholly safe, among his friends and in the arms of ordered sound, as if the music were an intimate crystal heaven around and over them, a perfect barrier to paranatural forces.

But then the harpsichord came in challengingly, banishing cradled sleep, its sparkling and shivery ribbons of high sound propounding questions and gayly yet inflexibly commanding that they be answered. The harpsichord told Franz that the concert hall was every bit as much an escape as anything proposed on Beaver Street.

Before he knew what he was doing, though not until he knew well what he was feeling, Franz had got stoopingly to his feet and was edging out in front of Saul, intensely conscious yet regardless of the waves of shock, protest, and condemnation silently focused upon him from the audience—or so he fancied.

He only paused to bend his lips close to Saul's ear and say softly but very distinctly, "Tell Cal, but only after she's played the Brandenburg, that her music made me go to find the answer to the 607 Rhodes question," and then he was edging on quite rapidly, the back of his left hand very lightly brushing back to steady his course, his right hand an apologetic shield between himself and the sitters he passed in front of.

As he reached the end of the row, he looked back once and saw Saul's frowning and intensely speculative face, framed by his long brown hair, fixed upon him. Then he was hurrying up the aisle between the hostile rows, lashed on— as if by a whip strung with thousands of tiny diamonds—by the music of the harpsichord, which never faltered. He kept his gaze fixed steadily ahead.

He wondered why he'd said "the 607 Rhodes question" instead of "the question of whether paramentals are real", but then he realized it was because it was a question Cal had herself asked more than once and so might catch the drift of. In the street outside he resumed his sidewise and backward peerings, now somewhat randomized; yet he was conscious not so much of fear as of wariness, as if he were a savage on a mission in a concrete jungle, traveling along bottoms of perilously walled, rectilineal gorges. Having taken a deliberate plunge into danger, he felt almost cocky.

He headed over two blocks and then up Larkin, walking rapidly yet not noisily. The passersby were few. The gibbous moon was almost overhead. Up Turk a siren yelped some blocks away. He kept up his swiveling watch for the paramental of his binoculars and/or for Thibaut's ghost, perhaps a material ghost formed of Thibaut's floating ashy remains, or a portion of them. Such things might not be real, there still might be a natural explanation (or he might be crazy), but until he was sure of one or the other, it was only good sense to stay on guard.

Down Ellis the slot which held his favorite tree was black, but its streetside branch-ends were green in the white street lights.

He turned down Geary past dark shop fronts, two lighted bars, and the wide yawning mouth of the De Soto garage, home of the blue taxicabs, and came to the dingy white awning that marked 811.

Inside the lobby there were a couple of rough-looking male types sitting on the ledge of small hexagonal marble tiles below the two rows of brass mailboxes. Probably drunk. They followed him with their dull eyes as he took the elevator.

He got off at six and closed the two elevator doors quietly (the folding latticed and the solid one) and walked softly past the black window and the black broom-closet door, with its gaping round hole where the knob would have been, and stopped in front of his own door.

After listening a short while and hearing nothing, he unlocked it with two twists of his key and stepped inside, feeling a burst of excitement and fear. This time he did not switch on the bright ceiling light, but only stood listening and intent, waiting for his eyes to accommodate.

The room was full of darkness. Outside the open window the night was pale (dark gray, rather) with the moon and with the indirect glow of the city's lights. Moonlight was not yet coming into the room. Everything was very quiet except for the faint, distant rumbles and growls of traffic and the rushing of his blood. Suddenly there came through the pipes a solid, low roaring as someone turned on water a floor or two away. It stopped as suddenly and the inside silence returned.

Adventurously, Franz shut the door and felt his way along the wall and around the tall clothes cabinet, carefully avoiding the work-laden coffee table, to the head of his bed, where he turned on the light. He ran his gaze along his Scholar's Mistress, lying slim, dark and inscrutably silent against the wall, and on to the open casement window.

Two yards inside it, the large oblong of fluorescent red cardboard lay on the floor. He walked over and picked it up. It was jaggedly bent down the middle and a little ragged at corners. He shook his head, set it against the wall, and went back to the window. Two torn corners of cardboard were still tacked to the window sides. The drapes hung tidily. There were crumbles and tiny shreds of pale brownish paper on his narrow desk and the floor at his feet. He couldn't remember whether or not he'd cleaned up those from yesterday.

Conceivably a very strong gust of wind could have torn out the red cardboard, but wouldn't it also have disordered the drapes and blown the paper crumbs off his desk? He looked out to the red lights of the TV tower, thirteen of them small and steady, six brighter and flashing. Below, a mile closer, the dark hump of Corona Heights was outlined by the city's yellowish window and street lights and a few bright whites and greens in snaky curves. Again he shook his head.

He rapidly searched his place, this time not feeling foolish. In the closet and clothes cabinet he swung the hanging garments aside and glanced behind them. He noticed a pale-gray raincoat of Cal's from weeks back. He looked behind the shower curtain and under the bed.

On the table between the closet and bathroom doors lay his unopened mail. Topmost was a cancer drive letter from the hospital where Daisy had died. He frowned and momentarily narrowed his lips, his face compressed with pain. Beside the little pile were a small slate, some pieces of white chalk, and his prisms, with which he occasionally played with sunlight, splitting it into spectrums and into spectrums of spectrums. He called to his Scholar's Mistress, "We'll have you in gay clothes again, just like a rainbow, my dear, after all this is over."

He got a city map and a ruler and went to his couch, where he fished his broken binoculars out of his pocket and set them carefully on an unpiled edge of the coffee table. It gave him a feeling of safety to think that now the snout-faced paramental couldn't get to him without crossing broken glass, like that which they used to cement atop walls to keep out intruders—until he realized just how illogical that was.

He took out Smith's journal too and settled himself beside his Scholar's Mistress, spreading out the map. Then he opened the journal to de Castries' curse, marvelling again that it had so long eluded him, and reread the crucial portion:

The fulcrum (O) and the Cipher (A) shall be here, at his *beloved* 607 Rhodes. I'll be at rest in my appointed spot (1) under the Bishop's Seat, the heaviest ashes that he ever felt. Then when the weights are on at Sutro Mount (4) and Monkey Clay (5) [(4) + (1) = (5)] *BE his Life Squeezed Away.*

Now to work out, he told himself, this problem in black geometry, or would it be black physics? What had Byers said Klaas had said de Castries had called it? Oh yes, Neopythagorean metageometry.

Monkey Clay was the most incongruous item in the course, all right. Start there. Donaldus had maundered about simian and human clay, but that led nowhere. It ought to be a *place*, like Mount Sutro—or Corona Heights (under the Bishop's Seat). Clay was a street in San Francisco. But Monkey?

Franz's mind leapt from Monkey Clay to Monkey Wards. Why? He'd known a man who'd worked at Sears Roebuck's great rival and said he and some of his lowly co-workers called their company that.

Another leap, from Monkey Wards to the Monkey Block. Of course! The Monkey Block was the proudly derisive name of a huge old San Francisco apartment building, long torn down, where bohemians and artists had lived cheaply in the Roaring Twenties and the Depression years. Monkey short for the street it was on—Montgomery! Another San Francisco street, and one crosswise to Clay! (There was something more than that, but his mind hung fire and he couldn't wait.)

He excitedly laid the ruler on the flattened map between Mount Sutro and the intersection of Clay and Montgomery Streets in the north end of the financial district. He saw that the straight line so indicated went through the middle of Corona Heights! (And also rather close by the intersection of Geary and Hyde, he noted with a little grimace.)

He took a pencil from the coffee table and marked a small five at the Montgomery-Clay intersection, a four by Mount Sutro, and a one in the middle of Corona Heights. He noted that the straight line became like a balance or scales then (two lever arms) with the balancing point or fulcrum somewhere between Corona Heights and Montgomery-Clay. It even balanced mathematically: four plus one equals five—just as was noted in the curse before the final injunction. That miserable fulcrum (O), wherever it was, would surely be pressed to death by those two great lever arms ("Give me a place to stand and I will stomp the world to death." – Archimedes) just as that poor little lower-case "his" was crushed between that dreadful BE and the three big capitalized words.

Yes, that unfortunate (O) would surely be suffocated, compressed to a literal nothing, especially when "the weights" were "on". Now what—?

Suddenly it occurred to Franz that whatever had been the case in the past, the weights were certainly on *now*, with the TV tower standing three-legged on Mount Sutro and with Montgomery-Clay the location of the Transamerica Pyramid, San Francisco's tallest building! (The "something else" was that the Monkey Block had been torn down to clear a site first for a parking lot, then for the Transamerica Pyramid. Closer and closer!)

That was why the curse hadn't got Smith. He'd died before either structure had been built. The trap hadn't become set until *now*.

The Transamerica Pyramid and the 1,000-foot TV tower—those were crushers, all right.

But it was ridiculous to think that de Castries could have predicted the building of those structures. And in any case coincidence—lucky hits—was an adequate explanation. Pick any intersection in downtown San Francisco, and there was at least a fifty-percent chance of there being a high rise there, or nearby.

But why was he holding his breath then, why was there a faint roaring in his ears, why were his fingers cold and tingling? Why had de Castries told Klaas and Ricker that prescience, or foreknowledge, was possible at certain spots in mega-cities? Why had he named his book (it lay beside Franz now, a dirty gray) *Megapolisomancy*?

Whatever the truth behind, the weights certainly were on now, no question.

Which made it all the more important to find out the real location of that baffling 607 Rhodes where the old devil had lived (dragged out the tail end of his life) and Smith had asked his questions . . . and where, according to the curse, the ledger containing the Grand Cipher was hidden . . . and where the curse would be fulfilled. Really, it was quite like a detective story. By Dashiell Hammett? "X marks the spot" where the victim was (will be?) discovered, crushed to death? They'd put up a brass plaque at Bush and Stockton near where Brigid O'Shaunnesy had shot Miles Archer in Hammett's *The Maltese Falcon*, but there were no memorials for Thibaut de Castries, a real person. Where was the elusive X, or mystic (O)? Where *was* 607 Rhodes? Really, he should have asked Byers when he'd had the chance. Call him up now? No, he'd severed his connection there. Beaver Street was an area he didn't want to venture back to, even by phone. At least for now. But he left off poring over the map as futile.

His gaze fell on the 1927 San Francisco City Directory he'd ripped off that morning that formed the midsection of his Scholar's Mistress. Might as well finish that bit of research right now—find the name of this building, if it ever had one, if it had, indeed, become a listed hotel. He heaved the thick volume onto his lap and turned the dingily yellowed pages to the "Hotels" section. At another time he'd have been amused by the old advertisements for patent medicines and barber parlors.

He thought of all the searching around he'd done this morning at the Civic Center. It all seemed very far off now and quite naïve.

Let's see, the best way would be to search through the addresses, not for Geary Street—there'd be a lot of hotels on Geary—but for 811. There'd probably only be one of those, if any. He began running a fingernail down the first column rather slowly, but steadily.

He was on the next to the last column before he came to an 811. Yes, it was Geary too, all right. The name was . . . the Rhodes Hotel.

Before he realized why he was doing it, he had got up and gone out into the hall and closed his door. Then he knew why.

It was to see the number on the door, the small dark oblong on which was incised in pale gray, 607. He wanted to see it actually and to see his room from the outside (and incidentally disassociate himself from the curse, get off the target).

He got the feeling that if he knocked just now (as Clark Smith must have knocked so many times on this same door) Thibaut de Castries would open it, his sunk-cheeked face a webwork of fine gray wrinkles as if it had been sprinkled with fine ashes.

If he went in without knocking, it would be as he'd left it. But if he knocked, then the old spider would wake . . .

He felt vertigo, as if the building were beginning to lean over with him inside it, to rotate ever so slowly, at least at first . . . the feeling was like earthquake panic.

He had to orient himself at once, he told himself, to keep himself from falling over with 811. He went down the dark hall (the bulb inside the globe over the elevator door was still out) past the black broom closet, the black-painted window of the airshaft, the elevator itself, and softly up the stairs two flights, gripping the banister to keep his balance, and under the peaked skylight of the stairwell into the sinister black room that housed under a larger skylight the elevator's motor and relays, and so out onto the tarred and gravelled roof.

The stars were in the sky where they should be, though naturally dimmed somewhat by the glare of the gibbous moon, which was in the top of the sky a little to the south. Orion and Aldebaran climbed the east. Polaris was at his unchanging spot. All round about stretched the angular horizon, crenelated with high rises and skyscrapers marked rather sparsely with red warning and yellow window lights, as if somewhat aware of the need to conserve energy. The moderate wind was from the west.

His dizziness gone at least, Franz moved toward the back of the roof, past the mouths of the air shafts that were like walled square wells, and watchful for the low vent pipes covered with heavy wire netting that were so easy to trip over, until he stood at the roof's west edge above his room and Cal's. One of his hands rested on the low wall. Off a short way behind him was the air shaft that dropped straight down by the window he'd passed in the hall and the corresponding ones above and below it. Opening on the same shaft, he recalled, were the bathroom windows of another set of apartments and also a vertical row of quite small windows that could only let into the disused broom closets, originally to give them some light, he supposed. He looked west at the flashing reds of the TV tower and at the irregularly rounded darkness of the Heights. The wind freshened a little.

He thought at last, this is the Rhodes Hotel. I live at 607 Rhodes, the place I've hunted for everywhere else. There's really no mystery at all about it. Behind me is the Transamerica Pyramid (5). (He looked overshoulder at it where its single red light flashed bright and its lighted windows were as narrow as the holes in a business machine card.) In front of me (he turned back) are the TV tower (4) and the crowned and hunchbacked eminence (1) where the old spider king's ashes lie buried, as they say. And I am at the fulcrum (O) of the Curse.

As he fatalistically told himself that, the stars seemed to grow dimmer still, a sickly pallor, and he felt a sickness and a heaviness within himself and all around, as if the freshening wind had blown something malignant out of the west to this dark roof, as if some universal disease or cosmic pollution were spiralling from Corona Heights to the whole cityscape and so up to the stars, infecting even Orion and the Shield—as if with the stars' help he'd been getting things in place and now something was refusing to stay in its appointed spot, refusing to stay buried and forgotten, like Daisy's cancer, and interfering with the rule of number and order in the universe.

He heard a sudden scuffing and a scuttling sound behind him and he spun around. Nothing there, nothing that he could see, and yet . . .

He moved to the nearest air shaft and looked down. Moonlight penetrated it as far as his floor, where the little window to the broom closet was open. Below that, it was very dimly lit from two of the bathroom windows—indirect light seeping from the living rooms of those apartments. He heard a sound as of an animal snuffing, or was that his own heavy breathing reflected by the echoing sheetiron? And he fancied he saw (but it was very dim) something with rather too many limbs moving about, rapidly down and up.

He jerked his head back and then up, as if looking to the stars for help, but they seemed as lonely and uncaring as the very distant windows a lone man sees who is about to be murdered on a moor or sink into the Great Grimpen Marsh at dead of night. Panic seized him and he rushed back the way he'd come. As he passed through the black room of the elevator, the big copper switches snapped loudly and the relay arms clashed grindingly, hurrying his flight as if there were a monster snapping at his heels.

He got some control of himself going down the stairs, but on his own floor as he passed the black-painted window (near the dark ceiling globe) he got the feeling there was something supremely agile crouched against the other side of it, clinging in the air shaft, something midway between a black panther and a spider monkey, but perhaps as many-limbed as a spider and perhaps with the creviced, ashen face of Thibaut de Castries, about to burst in through the wire-toughened glass. And as he passed the black door of the broom closet, he remembered that small window opening from it into the shaft, that would not be too small for such a creature. And how the broom closet itself was right up against the wall that ran along the inside of his couch. How many of us in a big city, he asked himself, know anything about what lies in or just on the other side of the outer walls of our apartments, often the very wall against which we sleep?—as hidden and unreachable as our internal organs. We can't even trust the walls that guard us.

In the hall, the broom closet door seemed suddenly to bulge. For a frantic moment he thought he'd left his keys in his room; then he had found them in his pocket and located the right one on the ring and got the door open and himself inside and the door double-locked behind him against whatever might have followed him from the roof.

But could he trust his room with its open window?— no matter how unreachable the latter was in theory. He searched the place again, this time finding himself impelled to view each volume of space. Even pulling the file drawers out and peering behind the folders did not make him feel embarrassed. He searched his clothes cabinet last and so thoroughly that he discovered on its floor against the wall behind some boots an unopened bottle of kirschwasser he must have squirreled away there over a year ago when he was still drinking.

He glanced toward the window with its crumbles of ancient paper and found himself picturing de Castries when he'd lived here. The old spider had doubtless sat before the window for long hours, viewing his grave-to-be on Corona Heights with forested Mount Sutro beyond. And had he previsioned the tower that would rise there? The old spiritualists and occultists believed that the astral remains, the odic dust, of a person lingered on in rooms where he'd lived.

If only there were someone to talk to and free him from these morbid thoughts! If only Cal and the others would get back from the concert. But his wristwatch indicated that it was only a few minutes past nine. Hard to believe his room searches and roof visit had taken so little time, but the second hand of his wristwatch was sweeping around steadily in almost imperceptibly tiny jerks.

The thought of the lonely hours ahead made him feel desperate, and the bottle in his hand with its white promise of oblivion tempted him, but the dread of what might happen when he had made himself unarousable was still greater.

He set the cherry brandy down beside yesterday's mail, also still unopened, and his prisms and slate. He'd thought the last was blank, but now he fancied he saw faint marks on it. He took it and the chalk and prisms lying on it over to the lamp at the head of his couch. He'd thought of switching on the 200-watt ceiling light, but somehow he didn't like the idea of having his window stand out that glaringly bright, perhaps for a watcher on Corona Heights.

There *were* spidery chalk marks on the slate—a half dozen faint triangles that narrowed toward the downward corner, as if someone or some force had been lightly outlining (the chalk perhaps moving like the planchette of a Ouija board) the snouted face of his paramental. And now the chalk and one of the prisms *were* jumping about like planchettes, his hands holding the slate were shaking so.

His mind was almost paralyzed, almost blanked, by sudden fear, but a free corner of it was thinking how a white five-pointed star with one point directed *upward* (or outward) is supposed in witchcraft to protect a room from the entry of evil spirits, as if the entity would be spiked on the star's upward (or outward) point, and so he was hardly surprised when he found that he'd put down the slate on the end of his piled coffee table and was chalking such stars on the sills of his windows, the open one and the locked one in the bathroom, and above his door. He felt distantly ridiculous but didn't even consider not completing the stars. In fact, his imagination ran on to the possibility of even more secret passageways and hiding places in the building than the air shafts and broom closets (mightn't there have been a dumb-waiter or a laundry chute in the Rhodes Hotel?—and who knows what auxiliary doors?), and he became bothered that he couldn't inspect the back walls of the closet and clothes cabinet more clearly, and in the end he closed the doors of both and chalked a star above them—and a small star above the transom.

He was considering chalking one more star on the wall by his couch, where it abutted the broom closet in the hall, when there sounded at his door a sharp *knock-knock*. He put on the chain before he opened it the two inches which that allowed. Half of a toothy mouth and a large brown eye were grinning up at him across the chain and a voice saying, "E' chess?"

Franz quickly unhooked the chain and opened the door eagerly. He was vastly relieved to have a familiar person with him, sharply disappointed that it was someone with whom he could hardly communicate at all—certainly not that stuff crowding his mind, yet consoled by the thought that at least they shared the language of chess—and chess would at least pass some time, he hoped.

Fernando came in beaming, though frowning questioningly a moment at the chain, and then again at Franz when he quickly reclosed and double-locked the door.

In answer Franz offered him a drink. Fernando's black eyebrows went up at sight of the square bottle, and he smiled wider and nodded, but when Franz had opened the bottle and poured him a small wine glass, he hesitated, asking with his mobile features and expressive hands why Franz wasn't drinking.

As the simplest solution, Franz poured himself a bit in another wine glass, hiding with his fingers how little, and tilted the glass until the aromatic liquid wet his closed lips. He offered Fernando a second drink, but the latter pointed towards the chessmen, then at his head, which he shook smilingly.

Franz set the chessboard somewhat precariously on top of the piled folders on the coffee table and sat down on the bed. Fernando looked somewhat dubiously at the arrangement, then shrugged and smiled, drew up a chair and sat down opposite. He got the white pawn, and when they'd set up the men, he opened confidently.

Franz made his moves quickly too. He found himself almost automatically resuming the "on guard" routine he'd employed at Beaver Street while listening to Byers. His watchful gaze would move from the end of the wall behind him to his clothes cabinet to the door, then, past a small bookcase and desk, pause at the window, then travel along his filing cabinets to the steam radiator and to the other end of the wall behind him, then start back again. He got the ghost of a bitter taste as he wet his lips—the kirschwasser.

Fernando won in twenty moves or so. He looked thoughtfully at Franz for a couple of moments, as if about to make some point about his indifferent play, but instead smiled and began to set up the men with colors reversed.

With deliberate recklessness Franz opened with the king's gambit. Fernando countered in the center with his queen's pawn. Despite the dangerous and chancy position, Franz found he couldn't concentrate on the game. He kept searching his mind for other precautions to take besides his visual guard. He strained his ears for sounds at the door and beyond the other partitions. He wished desperately that Fernando had more English, or weren't so deaf. The combination was simply too much.

And the time passed so slowly. The large hand of his wristwatch was frozen. It was like one of those moments at a drunken party, when you're on the verge of blackout, that seem to last forever. At this rate it would be ages before the concert was over.

And then it occurred to him that he had no guarantee that Cal and the others would return at once. People generally went to bars or restaurants after performances, to celebrate or talk.

He was faintly aware of Fernando studying him between the moves.

Of course he could go back to the concert himself when Fernando left. But that wouldn't settle anything. He'd left the concert determined to solve the problem of de Castries' curse and all the strangeness that went with it. And at least he'd made progress. He'd already answered the literal 607 Rhodes question, but of course he'd meant a lot more than that when he'd spoken to Saul.

But how could he find the answer to the whole thing anyway? Serious psychic or occult research was a matter of elaborate preparation and study, using delicate, carefully checked-out instruments, or at any rate sensitive, trained people salted by previous experience: mediums, sensitives, telepaths, clairvoyants and such—who'd proved themselves with Rhine cards and what not. What could he hope to do just by himself in one evening? What had he been thinking of when he'd walked out on Cal's concert and left her that message?

Yet somehow he had the feeling that all the psychical research experts and their massed experience wouldn't really be a bit of help to him now. Any more than the science experts would be with their incredibly refined electronic and radionic detectors and photography and what not. That amid all the fields of the occult and fringe-occult that were flourishing today—witchcraft, astrology, biofeedback, dowsing, psychokinesis, auras, acupuncture, exploratory LSD trips, loops in the time stream, astrology (much of them surely fake, some of them maybe real)—this that was happening to him was altogether different.

He pictured himself going back to the concert, and he didn't like the picture. Very faintly, he seemed to hear the swift, glittery music of a harpsichord, still luring and lashing him on imperiously.

Fernando cleared his throat. Franz realized he'd overlooked a mate in three moves and had lost the second game in as few moves as the first. He automatically started to set up the pieces for a third.

Fernando's hand, palm down in an emphatic "No," prevented him. Franz looked up.

Fernando was looking intently at him. The Peruvian frowned and shook a finger at Franz, indicating he was concerned about him. Then he pointed at the chessboard, then at his own head, touching his temple. Then he shook his head decisively, frowning and pointing toward Franz again.

Franz got the message: "Your mind is not on the game." He nodded.

Fernando stood up, pushing his chair out of the way, and pantomimed a man afraid of something that was after him. Crouching a little, he kept looking around, much as Franz had been doing but more obviously. He kept turning and looking suddenly behind him, now in one direction, now the other, his face big-eyed and fearful.

Franz nodded that he got it.

Fernando moved around the room, darting quick glances at the hall door and the window. While looking in another direction, he rapped loudly on the radiator with his clenched fists, then instantly gave a great start and backed off from it.

A man very afraid of something, startled by sudden noises, that must mean. Franz nodded again. Fernando did the same thing with the bathroom door and with the nearby wall. After rapping on the latter he stared at Franz and said, "*Hay hechicería. Hechicería ocultada en murallas.*"

What had Cal said that meant? "Witchcraft, witchcraft hidden in walls." Franz recalled his own wonderings about secret doors and chutes and passageways. But did Fernando mean it literally or figuratively? Franz nodded, but pursed his lips and otherwise tried to put on a questioning look.

Fernando appeared to notice the chalked stars for the first time. White on pale woodwork, they weren't easy to see. His eyebrows went up and he smiled understandingly at Franz and nodded approvingly. He indicated the stars and then held his hands out, palms flat and away from him, at the window and doors, as if keeping something out, holding it at bay—meanwhile continuing to nod approvingly.

"*Bueno,*" he said.

Franz nodded, at the same time marvelling at the fear that had led him to snatch at such an irrational protective device, one that the superstition-sodden (?) Fernando understood instantly—stars among the graffiti on Corona

Heights. Could they have been intended to keep dead bones at rest and ashes quiet? Had *Byers* sprayed them there?

He stood up and went to the table and offered Fernando another drink, uncapping the bottle, but the latter refused it with a short crosswise wave of his hand, palm down, and crossed to where Franz had been and rapped on the wall behind the couch and turning toward Franz repeated, "*Hechicería ocultada en muralla!*"

Franz looked at him questioningly. But the Peruvian only bowed his head and put three fingers to his forehead, symbolizing thought (and possibly the Peruvian was actually thinking too).

Then Fernando looked up with an air of revelation, took the chalk from the slate beside the chessboard, and drew on the wall a five-pointed star, larger and more conspicuous and better than any of Franz's.

"*Bueno*," Fernando said again, nodding. Then he thought again, or seemed to think, using the same gesture, and, when he was done, went quickly to the hall door and pantomimed himself going away and coming back, and then looked at Franz solicitously, lifting his eyebrows, as if to say, "You'll be all right in the meantime?"

Rather bemused by the pantomime and feeling suddenly quite weary, Franz nodded with a smile and (thinking of the star Fernando had drawn and the feeling of fellowship it had given him) said, "*Gracias.*"

Fernando nodded with a like smile, unbolted the door and went out, shutting the door behind him. A little later Franz heard the elevator stop at his floor, its doors open and close, and go droning down. His ears and eyes were still on guard, tracking the faintest sounds and slightest sights, but tiredly, almost protestingly. Despite all the day's shocks and surprises, his evening mind (slave of his body's chemistry) was taking over. Presumably Fernando had gone somewhere—but why? to fetch what?—and eventually would come back as he'd pantomimed—but how soon? and again why? Franz didn't much care. He began automatically to tidy around him.

Soon he sat down with a weary sigh on the side of his bed and stared at the incredibly piled and crowded coffee table, wondering where to start. At the bottom was his neatly layered current writing work, which he'd hardly looked at or thought of since day before yesterday. Atop that were the phone on its long cord, his broken binoculars, his big tar-blackened, overflowing ashtray (but he hadn't smoked since he'd got in tonight and wasn't moved to now), the chessboard with its men half set up, beside it the flat slate scattered with its chalks, his prisms, and some captured chess pieces, and finally the tiny wine glasses and the square bottle of kirschwasser, still uncapped, where he'd set it down after offering it a last time to Fernando.

Gradually the whole jumbled arrangement began to seem drolly amusing to Franz, quite beyond dealing with. Although his eyes and ears were still tracking automatically (and kept on doing so), he almost giggled weakly. His evening mind invariably had its silly side, a tendency toward puns and oddly mixed clichés, and faintly psychotic epigrams— foolishness born of fatigue. He recalled how neatly the psychologist F.C. MacKnight had described the transition from waking to sleeping: the mind's short logical daytime steps becoming longer by degrees, each mental jump a little more far-fetched and wild, until (with never a break) they were utterly unpredictable giant strides and one was dreaming.

He picked up the city map from where he'd left it spread on his bed, and without folding it he laid it as if it were a coverlet atop the clutter on the coffee table.

"Go to sleep, little junk pile," he said with humorous tenderness.

And he laid the ruler he'd been using on top of that, like a magician relinquishing his wand.

Then (his ears and eyes still doing their guard rounds) he half turned to the wall where Fernando had chalked the star and began to put his books to bed too, as he had the mess on the coffee table, tucking in his Scholar's Mistress for the night, as it were—a homely operation upon familiar things that was the perfect antidote even to wildest fears.

Upon the yellowed, brown-edged pages of *Megapolisomancy*—the section about "electro-mephitic city-stuff"—he gently laid Smith's journal, open at the curse.

"You're very pale, my dear," he observed (the rice paper), "and yet the left-hand side of your face has all those very odd black beauty marks, a whole page of them. Dream of a lovely Satanist party in full evening dress, all black and white like *Marienbad*, in an angel-food ballroom with creamy slim borzois stepping about like courteous giant spiders."

He touched a shoulder that was chiefly Lovecraft's *Outsider*, its large, forty-year-old Winnebago Eggshell pages open at "The Thing on the Doorstep". He murmured to his mistress, "Don't deliquesce now, dear, like poor Asenath Waite. Remember, you've got no dental work (that I know of) by which you could be positively identified." He glanced at the other shoulder: coverless, crumble-edged *Wonder Stories* and *Weird Tales* with Smith's "The Disinterment of Venus" spread at the top. "That's a far better way to go," he commented. "All rosy marble under the worms and mold."

The chest was Ms. Lettland's monumental book, rather appropriately open at that mysterious, provocative, and question-raising chapter. "The Mammary Mystique: Cold as . . . " He thought of the feminist author's strange disappearance in Seattle. Now no one ever could know her further answers.

His fingers trailed across the rather slender black, gray-mottled waist made of James's ghost stories—the book had once been thoroughly rained on and then been laboriously dried out, page by forever wrinkled, discolored page—and he straightened a little the stolen city directory (representing hips), still open at the hotels section, saying quietly, "There, that'll be more comfortable for you. You know, dear friend, you're doubly 607 Rhodes now," and wondered rather dully what he meant by that.

He heard the elevator stop outside and its doors open, but didn't hear it going off again. He waited tautly, but there was no knock at his door, no footsteps in the hall that he could hear. There came from somewhere through the wall the faint jar of a stubborn door being quietly opened or closed, then nothing more of that.

He touched *The Spider Glyph in Time* where it was lying just below the directory. Earlier in the day his Scholar's Mistress had been lying on her face, but now on her back. He mused a moment (what had Lettland said?) as to why the exterior female genitalia were thought of as a spider. The tendrilled blot of hair? The mouth that opened vertically like a spider's jaws instead of horizontally like the human face's lips or the labia of the China-girls of sailors' legendry? Old fever-racked Santos-Lobos suggested it involved the time to spin a web, the spider's clock. And what a charming cranny for a cobweb.

His feather-touching fingers moved on to *Knochenmäd-chen im Pelze mit Peitsche)*—more of the dark hairiness, now changing to soft fur (furs, rather) wrapping the skeleton girls'—and *Ames et Fantômes de Douleur*, the other thigh; de Sade (or his posthumous counterfeiter), tiring of the flesh, had really wanted to make the mind scream and the angels sob; shouldn't *The Ghosts of Pain* be *The Agonies of Ghosts*?

That book, taken along with Masoch's *Skeleton Girls in Furs* (*with Whips*), made him think of what a wealth of death was here under his questing hands. Lovecraft dying quite swiftly in 1937, writing enthusiastically until the end, taking notes on his last sensations. (Did he see any paramentals then?) Smith going more slowly some quarter century later, his brain nibbled by little strokes. Santos-Lobos burned by his fevers to a thinking cinder. And was vanished Lettland dead? Montague there (his *White Tape* made a knee, only its paper was getting yellow) drowning by emphysema while he still wrote footnotes upon our self-suffocating culture.

Death and the fear of death! Franz recalled how deeply Lovecraft's "The Colour Out of Space" had depressed him when he'd read it in his teens—the New England farmer and his family rotting away alive, poisoned by radioactives from the ends of the universe. Yet at the same time it had been so fascinating. What was the whole literature of supernatural horror but an essay to make death itself exciting?—wonder and strangeness to life's very end. But even as he thought that, he realized how tired he was. Tired, depressed, and morbid—the unpleasant aspects of his evening mind, the dark side of its coin.

He finished tucking in his Scholar's Mistress—Prof. Nostig's *The Subliminal Occult* ("You disposed of Kirlian photography, doctor, but could you do as well with the paranatural?"), the copies of *Gnostica* (any relation to Prof. Nostig?), *The Mauritzius Case* (did Etzel Andergast see paramentals in Berlin?—and Waramme smokier ones in Chicago?), *Hecate, or the Future of Witchcraft* by Yeats, and *Journey to the End of Night* ("And to your toes, my dear")—and wearily stretched himself out beside her, still stubbornly watchful for the tiniest suspicious sounds and sights. It occurred to him how he had come home to her at night as to a real wife or woman, to be relaxed and comforted after all the tensions, trials, and dangers (remember, they were still there!) of the day.

It occurred to him that he could probably still catch the Brandenburg Fifth if he sprang up and hurried, but he was too inert even to stir—to do anything except stay awake and on guard until Cal and Gun and Saul returned.

The shaded light at the head of his bed fluctuated a little, dimming, then brightening sharply, then dimming again as if the bulb were getting very old, but he was much too weary to get up and replace it or even just turn on another light. Besides, he didn't want his window too brightly lit for something on Corona Heights (might still be there instead of here—who knew?) to see.

He noted a faint, pale, gray glitter around the edges of the casement window—the westering gibbous moon at last beginning to peer in from above, swing past the southern high rise into full view. He felt the impulse to get up and take a last look at the TV tower, say good night to his slender, thousand-foot goddess attended by moon and stars, put her to bed too, as it were, say his last prayers, but the same weariness prevented him. Also, he didn't want to show himself to Corona Heights or look upon the dark blotch of that place ever again.

The light at the head of his bed shone steadily, but it did seem a shade dimmer than it had been before the fluctuation, or was that just the pall cast by his evening mind?

Forget that now. Forget it all. The world was a rotten place. This city was a mess, with its gimcrack high rises and trumpery skyscrapers. It had all tumbled down and burned in 1906 (at least everything around this building had)—and soon enough would again, and all the papers would be fed to the document-shredding machines, with or without the help of paramentals. (And was not humped, umber raw Corona Heights even now stirring?) And the entire world was just as bad, it was perishing of pollution, drowning and suffocating in chemical and atomic poisons, detergents and insecticides, industrial effluvia, smog, the stench of sulfuric acid, the quantities of steel, cement, aluminum ever bright, plastics and paper, gas and electron floods—electro-mephitic city-stuff indeed!—though the world hardly needed the paranatural to do it to death. It was blackly cancerous like Lovecraft's farm family slain by strange radioactives come by meteor from the end of nowhere.

But that was not the end. (He edged a little closer to his Scholar's Mistress.) The electro-mephitic sickness was spreading, had spread (had metastasized) from this world to everywhere. The universe was terminally diseased; it would die thermodynamically. Even the stars were infected. Who ever thought that those bright points of light meant anything? What were they but a swarm of phosphorescent fruit flies momentarily frozen in an utterly random pattern around a garbage planet?

He tried his best to "hear" the Brandenburg Fifth that Cal was playing, the vastly varied, infinitely orderly diamond streamers of quill-plucked sound that made it the parent of all piano concertos. But all was silence.

What was the use of life anyhow? He had laboriously recovered from his alcoholism only to face the Nameless One once more in a new triangular mask. Effort wasted, he told himself now. In fact, he would have reached out and taken a bitter, stinging drink from the square bottle, except he was too tired to make the effort. He was an old fool to think Cal cared for him, as much a fool as Byers with his camp Chinese swinger and his teen-agers, his kinky paradise of sexy, slim-fingered, groping cherubs.

Franz's gaze wandered to Daisy's painted, dark-nested face upon the wall, narrowed by perspective to slit eyes and a mouth that sneered above a tapering chin.

At that moment he began to hear a very faint scuffing in the wall, like that of a very large rat trying very hard to be quiet. From how far did it come? He couldn't tell. What were the first sounds of an earthquake like?—the ones only the dogs could hear. There came a somewhat louder scuff, then nothing more.

He remembered the relief he'd felt when cancer had lobotomized Daisy's brain and she had reached the unfeeling vegetable stage and the need to keep himself anesthetized with alcohol had become a shade less pressing.

The light behind his head arced brightly greenish white, fluttered, and went out. He started to sit up, but barely lifted a finger. The darkness in the room took forms like the Black Pictures of witchcraft, crowd-stupefying marvels, and Olympian horrors which Goya painted for himself in his old age, a very proper way to decorate a home. His lifted finger vaguely moved toward Fernando's blacked-out star, then dropped back. A small sob formed and faded in his throat. He snuggled close to his Scholar's Mistress, his fingers touching her Lovecraftian shoulder. He thought of how she was the only real person that he had. Darkness and sleep closed on him without a sound.

Time passed.

Franz dreamed of utter darkness and of a great, white, crackling, ripping noise, as of endless sheets of newsprint being crumpled and dozens of books being torn across at once and their stiff covers cracked and crushed—a paper pandemonium.

Despite that mighty noise, he next thought he woke very tranquilly into two rooms: this with the this-in-dream superimposed. He tried to make them come together. Daisy was lying peacefully beside him. Both he and she were very, very happy. They had talked last night and all was very well. Her slim, silken, dry fingers touched his cheek and neck.

With a cold plunge of feelings, the suspicion came to him that she was dead. The touching fingers moved reassuringly. There seemed to be almost too many of them. No, Daisy was not dead, but she was very sick. She was alive, but in the vegetable stage, mercifully tranquilized by her malignancy. Horrible, yet it was still a comfort to lie beside her. Her fingers were so very slim and silken dry, so very strong and many, all starting to grip tightly—they were not fingers but wiry black vines rooted inside her skull, growing in profusion out of her cavernous orbits, gushing luxuriantly out of the triangular hole between the nasal and the vomer bones, turning in tendrils from under her upper teeth so white, pushing insidiously and insistently, like grass from sidewalk cracks, out of her pale-brown cranium, bursting apart the squamous, sagittal, and *coronal* sutures.

Franz sat up with a convulsive start, gagging on his feelings, his heart pounding, cold sweat breaking from his forehead.

Moonlight was pouring in the casement window, making a long, coffin-size pool upon the carpeted floor beyond the coffee table, throwing the rest of the room into darker shadow by contrast.

He was fully clothed, his feet ached in his shoes.

He realized with enormous gratitude that he was truly awake at last, that Daisy and the vegetative horror that had destroyed her were both gone, vanished far swifter than smoke.

He found himself acutely aware of all the space around him: the cool air against his face and hands, the eight chief corners of this room, the slot outside the window shooting down six floors between this building and the next to basement level, the seventh floor and roof above, the hall on the other side of the wall behind him beyond the head of his bed, the broom closet on the other side of the wall beside him that held Daisy's picture and Fernando's star, and the air shaft beyond the broom closet.

And all his other sensations and all his thoughts seemed equally vivid and pristine. He told himself he had his morning mind again, all rinsed by sleep, fresh as sea air. How wonderful! He'd slept the whole night through (had Cal and the boys knocked softly at his door and gone shrugging and smiling away?) and now was waking an hour or so before dawn, just as the long astronomical twilight began, simply because he'd gone to sleep so early. Had Byers slept as well?—he doubted that, even with his skinny-slim, decadent soporifics.

But then he realized that the moonlight still streaming in, as it had started to before he slept, and pooling on the floor, proved that he'd only been asleep an hour or less.

His skin quivered a little, and the muscles of his legs grew tense, his whole body quickened as if in anticipation of . . . he didn't know what.

He felt a paralyzing touch on the back of his neck. Then the narrow, prickly dry vines (it felt—though they were fewer now) moved with a faint rustle through his lifted hairs past his ear to his right cheek and jaw. They were growing out of the wall . . . no . . . they were not vines, *they were the fingers of the narrow right hand of his Scholar's Mistress, who had sat up naked beside him*, a tall pale shape unfeatured in the smudging gloom. She had an aristocratically small, narrow face and head (black hair?), a long neck, imperially wide shoulders, an elegant, Empire-high waist, slender hips and long, long legs—very much the shape of the skeletal steel TV tower, a far slenderer Orion (with Rigel serving as a foot instead of knee).

The fingers on her right arm that was snaked around his neck now crept across his cheek and toward his lips, while she turned and leaned her face a little toward his. It was still featureless against the darkness, yet the question rose unbidden in his mind as to whether it was just such an intense look that the witch Asenath (Waite) Derby would have turned upon her husband Edward Derby when they were in bed, with old Ephraim Waite (Thibaut de Castries?) peering with her from her hypnotic eyes.

She leaned her face closer still, the fingers of her right hand crept softly yet intrusively upward toward his nostrils and eye, while out of the gloom at her left side her other hand came weaving on its serpent-slender arm toward his face.

Shrinking away violently, he threw up his own left hand protectively and with a convulsive thrust of his right and of his legs against the mattress, he heaved his body across the coffee table, carrying all its heaped contents clattering and thudding and clashing (the glasses and binoculars) and cascading with him to the floor beyond, where (having turned over completely) he lay in the edge of the pool of moonlight, except for his head, which was in the shadow between it and the door. In turning over, his face had come close to the big ashtray as it was oversetting and to the gushing kirschwasser bottle, and he had gotten whiffs of stinking tobacco tar and stinging, bitter alcohol. He felt the hard shapes of chessmen under him. He was staring back wildly at the bed he'd quitted and for the moment he saw only darkness.

Then out of that darkness there lifted up, but not very high, the long pale shape of his Scholar's Mistress. She seemed to look about her like an animal, her small head dipping this way and that on its slender neck; then with a nerve-racking dry rustling sound she came writhing and scuttling swiftly after him across the low table and all its scattered and disordered stuff, her long-fingered hands reaching out far ahead of her on their wiry, pale arms. Even as he started to try to get to his feet, they closed upon his shoulder and side with a fearfully strong grip, and there flashed instantaneously across his mind a remembered line of poetry—"Ghosts are we, but with skeletons of steel."

With a surge of strength born of his terror he tore himself free of the trapping hands. But they had prevented him from rising, with the result that he only heaved over again through the moonlight pool and lay on his back, threshing, in its far edge, his head still in shadow.

Papers and chessmen and the ashtray's contents scattered further and flew. A wine glass crunched as his heel hit it. The dumped phone began to beep like a pedantic, furious mouse; from some near street a siren started to yelp like dogs being tortured; there was a great ripping noise as in his dream—the scattered papers churned and rose in seeming shreds a little from the floor—and through it all there sounded deep-throated, rasping screams which were Franz's own.

His Scholar's Mistress came twisting and hitching into the moonlight. Her face was still shadowed, but he could see that *her thin, wide-shouldered body was apparently formed solely of crumpled, crushed, and tightly compacted paper,* mottled pale brown and yellowish with age, as if made up of the chewed pages of all the magazines and books that had formed her on the bed, while about the back from her shadowed face there streamed black hair. (The books' shredded covers?) Her wiry limbs in particular seemed to be made up entirely of very tightly twisted and braided pale brown paper as she darted toward him with terrible swiftness and threw them around him, pinioning his own arms (and her long legs scissoring about his) despite all his flailings and convulsive kickings while, utterly winded by his screaming, he gasped and mewed.

Then she twisted her head around and up, so that the moonlight struck her face. It was narrow and tapering, shaped somewhat like a fox's or a weasel's, formed like the rest of her of fiercely compacted paper, constrictedly humped and creviced, but layered over in this area with dead white (the rice paper?) speckled or pocked everywhere with a rash of irregular small black marks. It had no eyes, although it seemed to stare into his brain and heart. It had no nose. (Was *this* the Noseless One?) It had no mouth— but then the long chin began to twitch and lift a little like a beast's snout, and he saw that it was open at the end.

The cables of the braided arms and legs twisted around him tighter; and the face, going into shadow again, moved silently down toward his; and all that Franz could do was strain his own face back and away.

He saw on the black ceiling, above the dipping muzzle and black hair, a little patch of soft, harmonious, ghostly colors—the pastel spectrum of moonlight, cast by one of his prisms lying in the pool on the floor.

The dry, rough, hard face pressed against his, blocking his mouth, squeezing his nostrils; the snout dug itself into his neck. He felt a crushing, incalculably great weight upon him. (The TV tower and the Transamerican! And the stars?) And filling his mouth and nose, the bone-dry, bitter dust of Thibaut de Castries.

At that instant the room was flooded with bright, white light; and, as if it were an injected instant stimulant, he was able to twist his face away from the rugose horror and his shoulders halfway around.

The door to the hall was open wide, a key still in the lock. Cal was standing on the threshold, her back against the jamb, a finger of her right hand touching the light switch. She was panting, as if she'd been running hard. She was still wearing her white concert dress and over it her black velvet coat, hanging open. She was looking a little above and beyond him with an expression of incredulous horror.

Then her finger dropped away from the light switch as her whole body slowly slid downward, bending only at the knees. Her back stayed very straight against the jamb, her shoulders were erect, her chin was high, her horror-filled eyes did not once blink. Then when she had gone down on her haunches, like a witchdoctor, her eyes grew wider still with righteous anger, she tucked in her chin and put on her nastiest professional look, and in a harsh voice Franz had never heard her use before, she said:

"In the names of Bach, Mozart, and Beethoven, the names of Pythagoras, Newton, and Einstein, by Bertrand Russell, William James, and Eustace Hayden, begone! All inharmonious and disorderly shapes and forces, depart at once!"

As she was speaking, the papers all around Franz (he could see now that they *were* shredded) lifted up cracklingly; the grips upon his arms and legs loosened so that he was able to inch toward Cal while violently threshing his half-freed limbs. Midway in her eccentric exorcism, the pale shreds began to churn violently and suddenly were multiplied tenfold in numbers (all restraints on him as suddenly gone) so that, at the end, he was crawling toward her through a thick paper snowstorm.

The innumerable-seeming shreds sank rustlingly all around him to the floor. He laid his head in her lap where she now sat erect in the doorway, half in, half out, and he lay there gasping, one hand clutching her waist, the other thrown out as far as he could reach into the hallway as if to mark on the carpet the point of farthest advance. He felt Cal's reassuring fingers on his cheek, while her other hand absently brushed scraps of paper from his coat.

He heard Gun say urgently, "Cal, are you all right? Franz!" Then Saul: "What the hell's happened to his room?" Then Gun again: "My God, it looks like his whole library'd been through a document shredder," but all that he could see of them were shoes and legs. How odd. There was a third pair—brown denim pants, and brown, scuffled shoes, rather small; of course, Fernando.

Doors opened down the hall and heads thrust out. The elevator doors opened and Dorotea and Bonita hurried out, their faces anxious and eager. But what Franz found himself looking at, because it really puzzled him, was a score or more of dusty corrugated cartons neatly piled along the wall of the hall opposite the broom closet and with them three old suitcases and a small trunk.

Saul had knelt down beside him and was professionally touching his wrists and chest, drawing back his eyelids with a light touch to check the pupils, not saying anything. Then he nodded reassuringly to Cal.

Franz managed an inquiring look. Saul smiled at him easily and said, "You know, Franz, Cal left that concert like a bat out of hell. She took her bows with the other soloists, and she waited for the conductor to take his, but then she grabbed up her coat—she'd brought it on stage during the second intermission and laid it on the bench beside her (I'd given her your message)—and she took off straight through the audience. You thought you'd offended them by leaving at the start. Believe me, it was nothing to the way she treated 'em! By the time we caught sight of her again, she was stopping a taxi by running out into the street in front of it. If we'd have been a bit slower, she'd have ditched us. As it was, she grudged us the time it took us to get in."

"And then she got ahead of us again when we each thought the other would pay the cab driver," Gun took up over his shoulder from where he stood inside the room at the edge of the great drift of shredded paper and stuff, as if hesitant to disturb it. "When we got inside she'd run up the stairs. By then the elevator had come down, so we took it, but she beat us anyway. Say, Franz," he asked, pointing, "who chalked that big star on your wall over the bed?"

At that question, Franz saw the small, brown, scuffed shoes step out decisively, kicking through the paper snow. Once again Fernando loudly rapped the wall above the bed, as if for attention, and turned and said authoritatively, "*Hechicería ocultada en muralla!*"

"Witchcraft hidden in the wall," Franz translated, rather like a child trying to prove he's not sick. Cal touched his lips reprovingly, he should rest.

Fernando lifted a finger, as if to announce, "I will demonstrate," and came striding back, stepped carefully past Cal and Franz in the doorway. He went quickly down the hall past Dorotea and Bonita and stopped in front of the broom closet door and turned around. Gun, who had followed inquisitively behind him, stopped too.

The dark Peruvian gestured from the shut doorway to the neatly stacked boxes twice and then took a couple of steps on his toes with knees bent. ("I moved them out. I did it quietly.") and took a big screwdriver out of his pants pocket and thrust it into the hole where the knob had been and gave it a twist and with it drew the black door open and then with a peremptory flourish of the screwdriver stepped inside.

Gun followed and looked in, reporting back to Franz and Cal, "He's got the whole little room cleared out. My God, it's dusty. Now he's kneeling by the wall that's the other side of the one he pounded on. There's a little shallow cupboard built into it low down. It's got a door. Fuses? No, it wouldn't be that, I'd think. Now he's using the screwdriver to open it like he did the other. Well, I'll be damned."

He backed away to let Fernando emerge, smiling triumphantly and carrying before his chest a rather large, rather thin gray book. He knelt by Franz and held it out to him, dramatically opening it. There was a puff of dust.

The two pages randomly revealed were covered from top to bottom, Franz saw, with unbroken lines of neatly yet crabbedly inked black astronomical and astrological signs and other cryptic symbols.

Franz reached out shakily toward it, then jerked his hand sharply back, as though afraid of getting his fingers burned.

It had to be the Fifty-Book, the Grand Cipher mentioned in *Megapolisomancy* and Smith's journal (B)—the ledger that Smith had once seen and that was an essential ingredient (A) of the Curse and that had been hidden almost forty years ago by old Thibaut de Castries to do its work at the fulcrum (O) at (Franz shuddered, glancing up at his door) 607 Rhodes.

∾

Next day, Gun incinerated the Grand Cipher at Franz's urgent entreaty, Cal and Saul concurring, but only after having it micro-filmed. Since then he'd fed it to his computers repeatedly, and let several semanticists and linguists study it variously, without the least progress toward breaking the code, if there is one. Recently he told the others, "It almost looks like Thibaut de Castries may have created that mathematical will o' the wisp—a set of completely random numbers." There did turn out to be exactly fifty symbols. Cal pointed out that fifty was the total number of faces of all the five Pythagorean or Platonic solids. But when asked what that led to, she could only shrug.

At first Gun and Saul couldn't help wondering whether Franz mightn't have torn up all his books and papers in some sort of short-term psychotic seizure. But they concluded it would have been an impossible task, at least to do in so short a time. "That stuff was shredded like oakum."

Gun also took apart Franz's binoculars (calling in his optical friend, who among other things had investigated and thoroughly debunked the famous Crystal Skull), but they found no trace of any gimmicking. The only noteworthy circumstance was the thoroughness with which the lenses and prisms had been smashed. "More oakum picking?"

Gun found one flaw in the detailed account Franz gave when he was up to it. "You simply can't see spectral colors in moonlight. The cones of the retina aren't that sensitive."

Franz replied somewhat sharply, "Most people can never see the green flash of the setting sun. Yet it's sometimes there."

Saul's comment was, "You've got to believe there's some sort of sense in everything that crazies say." "Crazies?" "All of us."

He and Gun still live at 811 Geary. They've encountered no further paramental phenomena, at least as yet.

The Luques are still there too. Dorotea is keeping the existence of the broom closets a secret, especially from the owner. "He'd make me e'try to rent them if he knew."

Fernando's story, as finally interpreted by her and Cal, was simply that he'd once noticed the little low cupboard in the broom closet while rearranging the boxes there to make space for additional ones and that it had stuck in his mind (*"Misterioso!"*) so that when *"Meestair Jueston"* had become haunted, he had remembered it and played a hunch.

The three Luques and the others (nine in all with Gun's and Saul's ladies) did eventually go for a picnic on Corona Heights after the winter's rains had turned it green. They even encountered the two little girls with the St. Bernard. Franz went a shade pale at that, but rallied quickly. Bonita played with them a while. All in all, they had an enjoyable time, but no one sat in the Bishop's Seat or hunted beneath it for signs of an old interment. Franz remarked, "I sometimes think the injunction not to move old bones is at the root of all the para . . . supernatural."

He tried to get in touch with Jaime Byers again, but phone calls and even letters went unanswered. Later he learned that the affluent poet and essayist, accompanied by Fa Lo Suee (and Shirl Soames too, apparently) had gone for an extended trip around the world.

"Somebody always does that at the end of a supernatural horror story," he commented sourly, with slightly forced humor.

He and Cal now share an apartment a little farther up Nob Hill. Though they haven't married, Franz swears he'll never live alone again. He never slept another night in Room 607.

As to what Cal heard and saw (and did) at the end, she says, "When I got to the third floor I heard Franz start to scream. I had his key out. There were all those bits of paper swirling around him like a whirlpool. At its center, just beyond him, they made a sort of skinny pillar with a nasty top. So I said (*pace* my father) the first things that came into my mind. As soon as I got Franz's message, I knew I must get to him as quickly as I could, but only after we'd played the Brandenburg."

Franz thinks the Brandenburg Fifth somehow saved him, along with Cal's subsequent quick action, but as to how, he has no theories. Cal only says, "I think it's fortunate Bach had a very mathematical mind and that Pythagoras was musical."

For a while Franz was very particular about never letting a book or magazine stay on his bed. But just the other day Cal found a straggling line of three there, on the side nearest the wall. She didn't touch them, but she did tell Franz about it. "I don't know if I could swing it again," she said. "So take care."

Cal says, "Everything's very chancy."

Story-telling, Wonder-questing,
Mortal Me: The Transformation of
The Pale Brown Thing *into*
Our Lady of Darkness

John Howard

One of Fritz Leiber's finest and best-known novels is *Our Lady of Darkness*. But that book did not appear out of nowhere. There was an earlier version: *The Pale Brown Thing,* published as a two-part serial in the issues for January and February 1977 of *The Magazine of Fantasy and Science Fiction* (*F&SF*). Later the same year, *Our Lady of Darkness* was published in hardcover, to be followed by other hardcover and paperback editions on both sides of the Atlantic. Bruce Byfield, in his so-far definitive study of Fritz Leiber's works *Witches of the Mind* (Necronomicon Press 1991) rightly devotes a fair amount of space to *Our Lady of Darkness*. Byfield describes the process by which the later book was expanded from the earlier novella as having been by the "addition of secondary narratives" (63). A little further on, he also tantalisingly quotes Leiber himself as saying that the two stories should really be regarded as one: " . . . the two texts should be regarded as the same story told at different times. If Franz's story is longer in *Our Lady of Darkness*, the reason is that he recalls more the second time he tells it."

The Pale Brown Thing was the latest then published of what turned out to be a succession of stories by Fritz Leiber which concerned aging, somewhat lonely men coming to terms with their place in the wider universe through an experience in their own apparently highly circumscribed and ordinary world, and which along with them is transformed in the process. These stories include "The Death of Princes", "Catch That Zeppelin!", "The Button Molder", and "Horrible Imaginings". The central character undergoes an experience, and encounter with the Other or the Outside after which nothing is quite the same again, and which enriches (even as it can terrify or suffuse with awe) the remaining time before his death.

It was another Leiber—Justin, Fritz Leiber's son—who wrote in his fascinating essay/memoir "Fritz Leiber and Eyes" that as his father's art "progressed in his growth in self-knowledge" he also "came to employ richer and more complicated forms, came to use himself and his artistic self-image in his art, came to play the mirror tricks of high art" (*Fantasy Commentator* 57 & 58 [2004], 93).

The Pale Brown Thing was a prime example of this, in which Leiber used his tricks to produce high art out of his life.

Fritz Leiber employed more than mere complication in his rich transformation of *The Pale Brown Thing* into *Our Lady of Darkness*. Several full "secondary narratives" were added, usually in the form of extended anecdotes by existing characters, and the interactions between the characters, all adding depth to the story. But the original story was also expanded by simply adding to descriptions, dialogue, thoughts, and so on—a few words here and there. The informality and immediacy—and therefore impact—of the narrative was already enhanced by Leiber's characteristic habit of making his characters "think out loud" and of displaying their thought-processes and additional thoughts in the form of bracketed phrases and individual words.

The additions cover a wide range. Many of them concern the story's San Francisco setting, and the history and topography of the city. Leiber further develops it into a character in its own right, rather than as simply the background for the story. Thus San Francisco takes on the stature of Arthur Machen's London and Wales, and H.P. Lovecraft's New England, in the verisimilitude of the setting, as well as the menace that it passively harbours or actively encourages.

In "Fritz Leiber and Eyes" Justin Leiber refers to his father as "a great student (professor?) of cities" (84). By the time that he was writing *The Pale Brown Thing* he possessed a pair of binoculars, and made great use of them. In the stories binoculars enhance the vision of the city and the surrounding world. (Leiber himself also used binoculars for his hobby of roof-top astronomy, which plays a major part in that great late story "The Button Molder"). We are shown that "Outward vision is inward vision" (84). Looking outwards into the city and the sky makes links with things that come to affect the inner being.

> There is the dark, eternally silent, unknown universe; there are the friend-enemy minds shouting and whispering their tales and always seeking the three miracles—that minds should really touch, or that the silent universe should speak, tell minds a story, or (perhaps the same thing) that there should be a story that works that is all hard facts, all reality, with no illusions and no fantasy; and lastly, there is lonely, story-telling wonder-questing, mortal me (*The Leiber Chronicles*, 524).

In one of the most eerie and unsettling passages in *The Pale Brown Thing* (left unchanged in *Our Lady of Darkness*) Franz Westen first sees, while using his binoculars, what he is up against, what has awakened. Looking at something, or someone, magnified, isn't necessarily a one-way process. Can it not also mean that the eyes are stared back into, and can become the means of entry into the mind? Mixing can occur. The outward vision is linked with the inward vision, and vice versa. Not only is self-knowledge gained and increased, but something from outside can get to know someone as well.

Thus in *Our Lady of Darkness* Fritz Leiber fleshes out the character of his narrator, Franz Westen. His almost symbiotic relationship with the city is developed, and Westen's inner state is further explored. Leiber mixes his art with reality in an even headier cocktail that it had been in *The Pale Brown Thing*. He had already been using his fiction as forms of therapy and catharsis, writing a lot because he had a lot to say about the death of his wife, his battles with alcohol, and now living alone in a great city, and coming to terms with age, loss, and death.

On a more obviously mundane level, we find out more about Westen's daily habits, and the web of friendships that form much of his world within the small world of his apartment building, as well as the city outside it. Westen has also acquired a regular writing job—that of novelising episodes of *Weird Underground*, an occult and fantastic TV series. Leiber mentions this aspect of Westen's life so many times that it is tempting to read more into it than simply the business of making Franz Westen into a still more credible character. (In his real life Leiber had also published a novelisation, *Tarzan and the Valley of Gold*, in 1966). Several times Westen contrasts the sort of scenario that he had to use from *Weird Underground* with the strange events that are happening in his own life.

Westen's friendships are explored in greater detail, especially those with Cal, and the rather Fafhrd and Gray Mouser-like Gunnar and Saul. Two extended episodes in *Our Lady of Darkness* (Chapters Four, Nine, and Ten, plus connecting passages) explore the complex relationships between Gunnar and Saul, the two men and Cal, and all three with Franz.

If *The Pale Brown Thing* is the protagonist Franz Westen telling the story for the first time, then the longer version, *Our Lady of Darkness*, is the story as told again later, expanded and amplified, with the addition of much "secondary" matter of all kinds. *The Pale Brown Thing* and *Our Lady of Darkness* are simply best regarded as being two versions of the same story. And it is the best way to regard the two versions as recollections of one main sequence of events, told at two different times. (Not unlike how the three Synoptic Gospels recount one basic story, in three ways from three viewpoints, for different audiences.) But the additions are not secondary in the sense of being second-rate or less important. They are secondary only in the sense that they are recollected and told later rather than sooner.

Events recalled first are not always what can turn out to be the most important, and later additions can have the effect of achieving a better balance, and of adding depth and understanding to the earlier version of the narrative. The later version may well represent, possibly, the "preferred" version, in the sense that the addition of later memories and impressions contribute to, and complete, what it is that needs to be recalled and put across.

The Pale Brown Thing is a viable and complete story in its own right, and worth knowing in addition to its longer version in *Our Lady of Darkness*. I have no idea whether or not Leiber did actually write *The Pale Brown Thing* first and then literally expanded it for subsequent book publication.

I am inclined to think that he did, as the additions can be seen to so obviously work in that way.

Although the remarks already quoted from Justin Leiber's essay "Fritz Leiber and Eyes" were clearly made in the context of the novel *The Big Time*—and the Change War stories in general—I think that they are appropriate for much else that Fritz Leiber wrote.

> Any dream may realise that it has a dreamer, but then the dreamer becomes a part of the dream, and the dream acquires another level of structure. But the dream that this sort of dreamer dreams is itself a still greater dream and so must have still another dreamer, and so on. High art plays endlessly on this paradox and its analogs. Like Eddison's *Worm*, it is always swallowing its own tale/tail (90).

In my view both *The Pale Brown Thing* and *Our Lady of Darkness* were certainly the highly structured dreams of a master. And the essay is itself a piece of work that swallows its own tale/tail, with its interpenetrating layers of exploration and meaning.

As has been mentioned, Fritz Leiber's fiction grew more personal, and sometimes even positively confessional, as he grew older, and the quantity of his work began to decline. But the quality certainly did not. *The Pale Brown Thing* and *Our Lady of Darkness* are two of Leiber's most personal stories. The narrator of both accounts of the story, Franz Westen, is a lightly-fictionalised version of Leiber himself. The San Francisco settings are taken from life, and there are many references to real people, both living and dead, some of whom Leiber knew personally and were friends. Leiber clearly enjoyed himself when he invented names for these characters. Some of this circle makes their appearances in the stories (but Leiber drew from the living ones).

At the beginning of his essay, Justin Leiber made the point that:

> When I talk with philosophers, linguists, and psychologists, I am often struck by the way in which not only arguments but whole phrases of their recent writings appear in their conversation. They are, or become, what they write.
>
> This can be disappointing unless I remind myself that people who don't write usually have much less to say, and they generally don't change their patter much from year to year.

Fritz Leiber wrote much, and did have much to say. He became what he wrote, and wrote what he became. And both were high art.

The additions to The Pale Brown Thing

I have listed the additions to *The Pale Brown Thing*, and how they dovetail into *Our Lady of Darkness*. It can be seen that, like a carefully built structure, *The Pale Brown Thing* has been partially dismantled, as it were, and new sections, of greater or shorter length, were skilfully inserted, leaving a new and integral whole. Both versions exist on their own terms, and the continued existence of the two versions is to be preferred. They both leave the presumably now complete body of Fritz Leiber's work enriched.

Page numbers referred to first are those for *Our Lady of Darkness*, following the UK Millington edition (which is identical to the 1978 Fontana paperback edition). Page numbers in brackets refer to this edition of *The Pale Brown Thing*. This version has no chapter divisions.

5   [Entire quotation from De Quincey].
7   l.7-14 (p.1): The waxing . . . Mount Diablo.
          l.19-24: An observer below . . . for months.
9   l.6-24 (p.2): The TV tower . . . another matter.
9/10   l.24-28/1-7: Faint dismal . . . to their jobs.
11   l.13-34 (p.3): [There is a more elaborate descrip-
          tion of the Sutro Tower]
14   l.4-6 (p.5): A sudden . . . freakish gust.
          l.20-29 (p.6): [No mention of *Weird Underground*.]
          l.30-34: But this . . . a trifle,
15   l.3ff: [Considerably expanded]
15/16   l.5-27/1-8: In the hall . . . knocked at 407.
16/17   l.23-35/1-25 (p.7): I came down . . . *The Flute*.
17/18   l.26-35/1-6: Franz told Cal . . . down easily
19   l.30-31 (p.8): What sort . . . he do?
19/20   l.32-36/1-2: There's absolutely . . . Egypt.
21   l.1-2 (p.9): [No mention of de Camp and Squires]
23   l.10-15 (p.11): But as . . . ahead!
23/27   [Chapter Four added]
29   l.18-20 (p.13): and humorously . . . those jinn.
          l.22-25: He had added . . . mailed it.
30   l.34-35 (p.14): Beyond . . . breathing.
33   l.6-9 (p.16): from the faintly . . . beyond them.
          l.17-21: He chucklingly . . . tourists.
34   l.16-17 (p.17): [No mention of *Weird Underground*.]
35   l-17-20 (p.18): Grace Cathedral . . . Cathedral Hill.
37   l.28-31 (p.20): But what . . . more sense.
38   l.18 (p.21): Really, he couldn't get home too soon.
          l.19-20: The far side . . . central city.
39   l.1-6: He thought . . . things alone.
          l.19-22: The neighbourhood . . . his pocket.
40/41   l.31-35/1-2 (p.23): Had he thrown . . . helpful scavenger.
          l.20-23: Remembering this . . . their words.

41/42	He was a tall man, ashen blonde, a fine-down amiable viking. [Capital V] [Deleted at this point in *Our Lady of Darkness* and used in the completely new Chapter Four]
45/46	l.36/1-4 (p.26): Saul's eyes . . . Mrs. Luque. l.16-17 (p.27): The nearest . . . the Potrero.
46/47	l.24-28/1-2: and at Twin Peaks . . . laughter.
48	l.9 (p.28): and the name . . . had one. l.17-32 (p.29): Gun and Saul . . . their orders.
49	l.17-18: They are both . . . have power. l.20-21: Music? . . . learn that. l.24: [No mention of *Weird Underground*.] l.25: Bonita protested, No! l.26: . . . and the more serious junk,
49/50	l.35-36/1-5 (p.30): Saul said . . . Her mother
51	l.7-end p.65/p.66 l.1-2 (p.31): Béla Szláwik/ Fernando . . . rating
66	l.6-13: From time . . . come early.
67	l.17 (p.32): The green dwarf and the spider. l.18-25: Passing a shaft . . . dead asleep l.27-36: For San Francisco . . . Aldebaran.
70	l.13-17 (p.34): Franz picked up . . . journal.
72	l.6-7 (p.36): that twentieth-century puritanic Poe from Providence, l.11-13: (And hadn't Lovecraft . . . by correspondence.
74	l.19-27 (p.38): Mostly not . . . steaming coffee.
75	l.10-14 (p.39): Oscar Wilde's . . . their titles
75/76	l.26-end/1-3: Scanning . . . drug-widened awareness.
77	l.14-17 (p.40): But White . . . Robert Ingersoll!
78	l.11-22 (p.41): It was she . . . unexpected sides. l.30-34: You know . . . was wondering.
80	l.13-20 (p.42): with a symphony . . . paper snow.
81	l.28-32 (p.43): the latter . . . elder brother.
82	l.19-23: though that last . . . hotels too.

82/83   l.35-36/1-2 (p.44): Then he tramped . . . believing that.
83   l.12-14 (p.45): thinking somewhat . . . compulsive life!
85   l.24-27 (p.47): and then stroll . . . suggested.
86   l.3-4: who was kneading . . . blonde hair.
           l.10-12: Nothing at all . . . charming.
           l.25-27 (p.48): And there . . . as lingam.
87   l.8-13: He perversely . . . for that matter.
           l.21-23: making itself . . . smog over it.
           l.24: and north in Marin County
           l.27-33: He found himself . . . of the Bay.
88   l.8-12 (p.49): It was funny . . . mind did.
           l.16-19: And the pale blue . . . punch-card.
           l.25-31: Why, he'd been . . . gilded cross.
92   l.15-21 (p.52): Approaching Beaver Street . . .
           the city.
           l.28-30: Cal had said . . . gold trim.
94   l.10-12 (p.54): Or something . . . some novelty?
           l.15-21: And he turned . . . now behind him.
           l.24-29: Franz recalled . . . with him.
97   l.9-11 (p.56): This pear wine . . . sun-kissed slopes.
98   l.30-36 (p.58): I went . . . and yesterday.
99   l.1-8: But even . . . Donaldus so!
100   l.5: . . . and Cal.
           l.14-19 (p.59): It helped too . . . filigree on it
101   l.7-12: Which is odd . . . never sure.
103/104   l.18-36/1-11 (p.61): Rapidly travelling . . . upon
           the scene.
104   l.28-36/p.105/p.106, l.1-4: Mention of Love-
           craft . . . culture and art.
107   l.8-end/p.108/p.109/p.110, l.1 (p.62): Of
           course . . . Donaldus continued,
110   l.16-21 (p.63): you know . . . Gabriel Jogand . . .
111   l.9-12: Unfortunately . . . very obvious.

179   l.5-6 (p.122): All her movements . . . and beautiful.
181   l.7-13 (p.124): He realized that . . . Our Lady
         of Darkness.
         l.18-22: He thought in . . . Corona Heights.
186   l.19-25 (p.128): Gun kept some . . . affair.)
187/188 l.34-36/1-5 (p.129): Gunnar's Ingrid . . . a
         grimmer period:
         l.20-23 (p.130): *The Hound of the Basker-*
         villes . . . into that.
188/189 l.34-36/1: The pillar flew . . . inches deep.
189   l.10-29: Once, in a . . . he lit a cigarette.

Acknowledgements

The publisher would like to thank the following people
for their assistance in the preparation of this volume:
Scott Connors, Emma Flynn, Will Hart, John Howard,
Meggan Kehrli, Justin Leiber, Xand Lourenco,
Ken Mackenzie, Jim Rockhill,
Donald Sidney-Fryer, and Jason Zerrillo.

The Pale Brown Thing
was first published in
The Magazine of Fantasy and Science Fiction
in January and February of 1977.

"Story-telling, Wonder-questing, Mortal Me"
was first published in
Fritz Leiber: Critical Essays, edited by Ben Szumskyj,
Mcfarland & Company, 2007

About the Author

Fritz Leiber was born in Chicago on 24 December 1910. Although trained as an actor, he made his name among the pages of the pulp magazines of the 1930s and '40s. After a brief correspondence with H. P. Lovecraft, Leiber began writing in earnest, penning classics of science fiction, fantasy, and horror, including *Conjure Wife*, the Hugo Award-winning *Ill Met in Lankhmar*, and the pioneering tale of urban supernaturalism "Smoke Ghost". Leiber passed away in San Francisco in 1992 at the age of eighty-one.

SWAN RIVER PRESS

Founded in 2003, Swan River Press is an independent publishing company, based in Dublin, Ireland, dedicated to gothic, supernatural, and fantastic literature. We specialise in limited edition hardbacks, publishing fiction from around the world with an emphasis on Ireland's contributions to the genre.

www.swanriverpress.ie

*"Handsome, beautifully made volumes . . .
altogether irresistible."*

– Michael Dirda, *Washington Post*

*"It [is] often down to small, independent, specialist presses
to keep the candle of horror fiction flickering . . ."*

– Darryl Jones, *Irish Times*

*"Swan River Press has emerged as one of the most inspiring
new presses over the past decade. Not only are the books
beautifully presented and professionally produced, but they
aspire consistently to high literary quality and originality,
ranging from current writers of supernatural/weird fiction
to rare or forgotten works by departed authors."*

– Peter Bell, *Ghosts & Scholars*

THE HOUSE ON
THE BORDERLAND

William Hope Hodgson

An exiled recluse, an ancient abode in the remote west of Ireland, nightly attacks by malevolent swine-things from a nearby pit, and cosmic vistas beyond time and space. *The House on the Borderland* has been praised by China Miéville, Terry Pratchett, and Clark Ashton Smith, while H. P. Lovecraft wrote, "Few can equal [Hodgson] in adumbrating the nearness of nameless forces and monstrous besieging entities through casual hints and significant details, or in conveying feelings of the spectral and abnormal."

"Almost from the moment that you hear the title," observes Alan Moore, "you are infected by the novel's weird charisma. Knock and enter at your own liability." *The House on the Borderland* remains one of Hodgson's most celebrated works. This new edition features an introduction by Alan Moore, an afterword by Iain Sinclair, and illustrations by John Coulthart.

"A summit of Cosmic horror.
Scary, disturbing and magical."

– Guillermo del Toro

"Swan River Press has produced the best version ever.
There is no need for any other."

– *Dead Reckonings*

WRITTEN BY DAYLIGHT

John Howard

Sunsets in a London suburb, and a transformation into an Earthly paradise; paths winding through a Transylvanian palace gardens, and an obsessed journey towards a Mediterranean dream; a city so ancient that even its total disappearance has been forgotten, and an island of shifting sands that can never be truly mapped . . . The vivid and diverse settings of these stories are façades obscuring reality for the exiles and outcasts who find their way into them. Seemingly born out of time and place, they seek the right routes to bring them to where they want to be, but there are many diversions on the way. In these stories of haunted landscapes and intimidating cities many possibilities confront the unwary, but there is usually only one choice to be made.

"Howard's work is both delicate and powerful."

– The Agony Column

*"If there is a unifying theme here it is the transience
of existence, from the individual to the social
and even the geographical . . . not only well-written
but also offer remarkable ideas."*

– Supernatural Tales

*"Most of these tales are so subtle as to defy
any category of the strange at all, but reward
re-reading and are all the greater for it."*

– The Pan Review

THE ANNIVERSARY
OF NEVER

Joel Lane

Joel Lane's award-winning stories have been widely praised, notably by other masters of weird fiction such as M. John Harrison, Graham Joyce, and Ramsey Campbell. His tales also regularly appeared in the "best of" annual anthologies of Ellen Datlow, Karl Edward Wagner, and Stephen Jones. With this posthumous collection, Lane continues his unflinching exploration of the human condition. "*The Anniversary of Never* is a group of tales concerned with the theme of the afterlife," observed Lane, "and the idea that we may enter the afterlife before death, or find parts of it in our world." These stories of love and death will burrow deep into the reader's mind and impregnate it with a vision often as bleak as the night is black.

*"Melancholy and bleak, the weird, often dark stories
in this slim, beautiful volume are a fitting coda
to Lane's life and work."*

– Ellen Datlow

*"A liminal collection whose ghost like state almost mimics
that of much of the material contained within its pages."*

– Black Static

*"Rich and varied forms of darkness
illuminated by the author's wit and intelligence."*

– Supernatural Tales